PERFECT
MISTAKE

CHECK OUT ALL THE BOOKS IN THE
NEW YORK TIMES BESTSELLING **PRIVATE**
AND **PRIVILEGE** SERIES BY KATE BRIAN

PRIVATE

INVITATION ONLY

UNTOUCHABLE

CONFESSIONS

INNER CIRCLE

LEGACY

AMBITION

REVELATION

PARADISE LOST

SUSPICION

———————————————————————————

PRIVILEGE

BEAUTIFUL DISASTER

PERFECT MISTAKE

PERFECT MISTAKE

A PRIVILEGE NOVEL

BY

KATE BRIAN

SIMON & SCHUSTER BFYR

New York   London   Toronto   Sydney

An imprint of Simon & Schuster Children's Publishing Division
1230 Avenue of the Americas, New York, NY 10020

 is a trademark of Simon & Schuster, Inc.
For information about special discounts for bulk purchases, please contact Simon
& Schuster Special Sales at 1-866-506-1949 or business@simonandschuster.com.
The Simon & Schuster Speakers Bureau can bring authors to your live event. For
more information or to book an event, contact the Simon & Schuster Speakers
Bureau at 1-866-248-3049 or visit our website at www.simonspeakers.com.

alloyentertainment
Produced by Alloy Entertainment
151 West 26th Street, New York, NY 10001

Book design by Andrea C. Uva
The text of this book is set in Adobe Garamond.
Manufactured in the United States of America
2 4 6 8 10 9 7 5 3 1
Library of Congress Control Number 2009931723
ISBN 978-1-4169-6761-3
ISBN 978-1-4169-8548-8 (eBook)

FIRST
EDITION

For Sharren, and all those who love when I write the crazies

HOW FAR WE'VE COME

The first thing Ariana Osgood noticed was Kaitlynn Nottingham's shoes—those gorgeous, brown leather Marc Jacobs wedge sandals. Then she let her gaze travel ever so slowly from her enemy's pedicured toes up her long, recently waxed legs. She took in the pressed shorts, the pink sweater, the perfectly cropped hair. Finally, finally she looked into Kaitlynn's eyes. Jade green, they gleamed with malevolence.

In moments of abject fury, Ariana Osgood's mind often went for the details. The things she could catalogue, analyze, compartmentalize. And her particular obsession was shoes. Where the hell had Kaitlynn gotten the money for Marc Jacobs wedge sandals?

But then, Ariana already knew the answer to this question: Kaitlynn had gotten the money from her. That one million dollars Ariana had wasted blood, sweat, and tears to raise—the one million dollars Kaitlynn was supposed to be using to start a new life in Australia—had, at least partially, been used to secure a new wardrobe, an expensive haircut, and some seriously killer shoes. All things that would help Kaitlynn blend in perfectly on the Atherton-Pryce Hall campus. *Ariana's* campus, where the two of them now stood, in the rapidly waning light of the late-summer evening, facing off amidst a hundred happily chatting prep schoolers.

"Are you okay, Ana?" Kaitlynn asked, tilting her head in faux concern. She had just introduced herself as Lillian Oswald. So very close to Ariana's mother's name, Lillian Osgood. Kaitlynn had clearly known this would get right under Ariana's skin. "You look a little faint."

"She's right, Ana," Brigit Rhygsted agreed, reaching for Ariana's arm. "Have you eaten anything since the race this morning? We should get you some food." She gestured to the far wall of the room, where a few guys were high-fiving one another. "There's a table over there full of crap I can't eat. Want me to get you something? Or maybe Lily can. I'm on a diet," she explained to Kaitlynn. "I probably shouldn't even go near it. I have no willpower at *all.*"

Ariana's fingers curled. It was almost funny, Brigit babbling about her struggles with food as if that were important right now. But then, she had no idea there was a serious battle of wills going on right in front of her. As far as she knew, "Ana Covington" and "Lillian Oswald" had never met before this moment.

"No, thank you. I'm fine," Ariana said through her teeth, lifting her chin to show Kaitlynn that she was not about to go weak at the very sight of her. Even though that was exactly what had happened the moment she'd spotted Kaitlynn on the crowded quad. The party continued to bubble and swell, but all Ariana could do was hug herself tightly in an attempt to quell her rage-induced trembling.

A few yards away, Palmer Liriano laughed and Ariana found him with her eyes, needing a moment of relief. He stood near a table of sandwiches and snacks, laughing along with two of his best friends, Christian Brooks and international pop star Landon Jacobs. Ariana focused on his handsome face, his carefree smile, the way the breeze tossed his black hair back from his forehead, hoping the glimpse of her crush—the guy she would soon be calling her boyfriend—would soothe her. But it didn't work.

Kaitlynn Nottingham was here. The only person on the planet who could obliterate Ariana's carefully laid plan for a new life—the person who had sworn she'd be on a plane to another country by tonight if Ariana gave her the money she needed—was instead here. On the Atherton-Pryce Hall campus. The place that was supposed to be Ariana's new home. Her sanctuary.

The enemy had invaded. Had used Ariana's money to worm her way into APH. And now that she was here, who knew what she was going to do next?

"I think she's right, Ana. Let's get you something to eat," Kaitlynn said pointedly, clasping Ariana's upper arm in her viselike grip. Ariana imagined her skin melting away under the girl's poisonous touch. "Come on. We'll grab a snack and get to know each other better."

For a moment, Ariana assumed Brigit would follow, but there was something exclusionary in Kaitlynn's tone, and Brigit's wide blue eyes showed that she'd picked up on it. When Ariana glanced over her shoulder at Brigit, the girl had already roped Adam Lazerri, a scholarship student who had just transferred to APH, into conversation.

Kaitlynn released Ariana in front of one of the snack tables and started to load up a clear glass plate with sweets. All around them, friends gabbed and gossiped; a few adventurous couples had created their own dance floor at the center of the circle of tables, and every now and then someone would throw out a cheer for Team Gold and half the crowd would cheer and whoop in response. Everyone was having fun, except Ariana.

"Before you can embarrass yourself asking all the obvious questions, let me answer them," Kaitlynn said lightly, addressing the wide array of fruit, cookies, cakes, and tarts rather than granting Ariana the courtesy of looking her in the eye. She spoke at a volume just loud enough for Ariana alone to hear. "I've signed over most of the money you gave me to secure my place in APH's junior class *and* in this exclusive dorm thing you and your new friends call Privilege House."

Ariana's rage swelled to nuclear levels. "No. You can't," she said under her breath. "You cannot be in Privilege House."

Not after all the work Ariana had done to get in. Not after she'd been forced to steal from her team to buy Kaitlynn's silence about her true identity. Not after rigging the crew race that morning to ensure Team Gold's victory. Privilege House was Ariana's plum. The shiny purple plum that she had won for herself—and for Palmer Liriano and Lexa Greene and the rest of her team. She had not gone to all that trouble so Kaitlynn Nottingham of all people could share in the spoils.

"Apparently I can," Kaitlynn said blithely, nibbling on a black-and-white cookie. "You'd be surprised how hard up the APH administration was for cash. Seems the recession hit this place where it hurts."

Ariana's fingernails dug into the flesh on her forearm. This was all too much to bear. Far too much to absorb over the space of two measly minutes. Her brain was still wrapping itself around the fact that Kaitlynn had lied to her about her plans to leave the country, and now she was supposed to accept the fact that the girl had duped her again? That she had forced Ariana to raise for her the very money that would buy her a spot in Ariana's life? And not only a spot, but a significant spot? The girl was going to be living in her dorm, amongst her friends. Ariana was going to have to see her, talk to her, deal with her every single day.

But there was no denying it. Kaitlynn was standing right there. Just six inches away. Enjoying her cookie and smiling at megastar Landon, Maria Stanzini's secret boyfriend, across the quad.

"Who's that?" Kaitlynn asked, popping a blueberry into her mouth. "He is absolutely munchable."

Ariana's vision began to prickle over with gray spots. Her throat closed and her skin burned. There was no air. She was outdoors on a beautiful, late-summer night, the breeze rustling the leaves on the ash and maple and cherry trees dotting the campus, but there was no air.

Breathe, Ariana. Just breathe.

In, one . . . two . . . three . . .
Out, one . . . two . . . three . . .
In, one . . . two . . . three . . .
Out, one . . . two . . . three . . .

"Oh my God. You're not *actually* going to faint, are you?" Kaitlynn asked in an amused tone, grabbing another blueberry.

Ariana blinked. The gray spots dissipated.

"No. I'm not going to faint." *Bitch,* she added silently.

"Good. Because we have some business to discuss," Kaitlynn said, nudging Ariana farther away from the table as a group of sophomores descended in search of a sugar rush. "I'm sure Grandma Covington is sending you some sort of weekly allowance. I think it's only fair we split it."

Ariana's jaw clenched so hard she was sure she heard a tooth crack. "Fair? How, exactly?"

"Well, because you never would have met Briana Leigh *or* Grandma C. if it weren't for me," Kaitlynn said matter-of-factly, choosing a strawberry from her plate and biting into it. "You wouldn't be here right now, masquerading as a millionaire, if it weren't for me. In fact, you should be glad I'm letting you keep any of it."

"Then why, exactly, are you?" Ariana asked, genuinely curious. Back when Ariana and Kaitlynn had been cellmates at the Brenda T. Trumbull Correctional Facility for Women, Ariana had thought she knew how Kaitlynn's mind worked—had thought she was sweet, innocent, guileless—but it had all turned out to be a ruse. At this point, the girl was a complete enigma.

Kaitlynn clucked her tongue and tilted her head again, giving Ariana the tiniest pout. Her lips were stained from the berry. "Because I want you here. And you can't exactly keep up the charade without cash now, can you?"

"You want me here," Ariana said dubiously.

Kaitlynn's eyes widened innocently. She looked almost hurt. "Of course I do, *Ana*. You're the only friend I've got." She hooked her arm around Ariana's in an affable way and looked out across the crowded party with her. Handsome boys in their well-worn APH T-shirts or broken-in oxfords chatted with fresh-faced girls in designer outfits, their laughter and babble mingling on the breeze. Overhead, white and gold paper lanterns bounced and swayed, hanging from poles set up in a circle around the party area. In the background, music played at a low volume from hidden speakers. Kaitlynn let out a contented sigh. "Can you believe how far we've come? A few months ago, would you ever have imagined this was possible?"

Ariana thought about the sterile cell they used to share at the Brenda T., about the better life she'd imagined for herself and Kaitlynn. Of course, back then she hadn't known Kaitlynn was a seriously evil girl who was going to use her to get that life.

"We've really done it, A. You and me. I'm not saying it was all champagne and roses, but we've done it."

Ariana didn't buy Kaitlynn's act for a second. They were never going to be friends. If Kaitlynn actually wanted Ariana here, it was for some reason other than friendship. Some dark, sadistic reason.

"You're sick, you know that, don't you?" Ariana said.

Kaitlynn glanced at Ariana out of the corner of her eye. "You're going to have to stop saying such ugly things to me, Ana, now that we're going to be besties again."

"Munchable? Besties? Who talks like that?" Ariana asked with a sneer.

"Lillian Oswald does," Kaitlynn said with a smile. "She has an endearingly innocent side. I've played that well before, no?"

Ariana stared her down, fuming at the reference to their past.

"You're going to give me that money," Kaitlynn said, giving Ariana's arm a squeeze. "You're going to play along. And as long as you do, we should both get exactly what we want out of this place."

"And if I don't?" Ariana asked.

Kaitlynn shook her head, amused. "Do you really have to ask?"

Brigit chose that moment to bounce over to them like a bunny on Red Bull.

"Hey guys! Christian's setting up *Rock Band* over by the chapel steps. He's on guitar and I'm on drums, but we need a singer. Landon's being all prima donna about it. You in?"

"I don't sing," Ariana replied flatly, forgetting for the moment that she was supposed to be ingratiating herself to these people. She was too busy trying not to explode.

"Seriously? Lexa said you guys used to duet for all the talent shows at camp," Brigit said, her brow creasing.

Ariana cursed her bad luck. Of course Briana Leigh sang in talent shows. The girl was the biggest exhibitionist Ariana had ever known, aside, perhaps, from Kiran Hayes, her former friend from her former life at Easton Academy.

Kaitlynn's brows arched at this news. "Do you have an old friend who goes here, Briana Leigh?" she said, clearly amused.

"Lexa Greene. They went to equestrian camp together back in the day," Brigit supplied helpfully.

Kaitlynn's grin widened. "How . . . *nice* for you, Ana."

Ariana bristled. She and Kaitlynn both knew that having someone at APH that knew the now-deceased Briana Leigh Covington was anything but nice.

"You have no idea," Ariana said, forcing a chipper tone. "It was *amazing* to see her, and now it's like we've never been apart," she added pointedly. Just so Kaitlynn would know that she had everything under control. "But I don't really sing anymore," she told Brigit.

Brigit frowned, fiddling with the colorful plastic bracelet that encircled her wrist. "Okay. What about you, Lillian?"

Kaitlynn shrugged, still holding Ariana's gaze. "I can carry a tune." She released Ariana and placed her heaping plate of food down on the table, hardly touched. "See you later, Ana!"

She twiddled her fingers as she turned and dove into the crowd with Brigit. Soon Landon and Adam had joined them and then, inevitably, Palmer gravitated over as well. Maria, Lexa, and Soomie Ahn were off somewhere, dealing with Lexa and Palmer's breakup. But if they had been there, Ariana was sure the three of them would have been holding court with Kaitlynn as well. Kaitlynn was just that pretty, just that magnetic, just that interesting.

And, infuriatingly, just that difficult to ditch.

ROOMIES

In the dark of night, dozens of students poured from various dorms and picked their way to the center of campus with their suitcases and trunks and backpacks. Atherton-Pryce Hall was constructed in a series of circles. The innermost green contained a bubbling fountain and was conscribed by class buildings, the offices, and the chapel. The next ring housed the dorms, and on the outskirts stood the liberal arts buildings, gymnasium, and playing fields.

Ariana joined the mass of students gathered around the fountain, an excited buzz filling the air. The giddy atmosphere filled Ariana with a sense of extreme satisfaction. They were all here because of her. Because she had sabotaged the other crew teams that morning. Not that she could ever tell anyone that. But still. She was their benefactor, and the thought made her feel all fizzy inside.

As she wove around the groups of gossiping girls, texting and talking at the same time, the smattering of boys laughing and conspiring and checking out the girls, she searched the shadowy faces of the crowd for Lexa, Maria, Soomie, and Brigit. But she kept an eye out for Kaitlynn as well. She wanted to find her friends before Kaitlynn found her.

"Ana! Over here!" Lexa called out.

Ariana's relieved smile lasted but a brief moment. Standing in a klatch near the wide stone rim of the burbling fountain were the four girls Ariana had come to call her friends over the past week—and Kaitlynn Nottingham. The girl was simply everywhere.

Gripping the handle on her trunk a bit tighter, Ariana slowly made her way over. Everyone was dressed down in baggy sweats and T-shirts, ready for the move and some all-night socializing in their new rooms. Even Soomie, who was always perfectly pressed and coiffed, had her glossy dark hair tied into two haphazard braids and wore a navy blue APH sweatshirt over jeans. Brigit was sipping some kind of smoothie, her short blond hair dancing in the breeze, and Maria was looking around distractedly, her light brown hair back in a messy bun, her Juilliard sweatshirt two sizes too big for her slight frame.

"Hi, ladies," Ariana said, plastering an excited grin to her face, even though all she wanted to do was tear Kaitlynn's hair from her scalp. Just then, Tahira Al Mahmood and Allison Rothaus, Ariana's other two least favorite people at APH, walked by, chatting obnoxiously on their cell phones as they tugged their huge trunks behind them. Ariana's shoulder muscles curled. It seemed like the enemies were proliferating. At least Tahira and Allison's third BFF, Zuri Tavengua, had been on Team Gray and would not moving into Privilege House.

"Hey, Ana, have you met Lily?" Maria asked, taking a break from nail chewing long enough to gesture at Kaitlynn. "She just transferred in too."

Ariana's smile stiffened. She did not turn to look at Kaitlynn. "We've met."

"Hi, Ana!" Kaitlynn said brightly, forcing Ariana to look at her.

Ariana met her gaze coolly. There was no way she was going to let Kaitlynn become part of her group. No way in hell.

"Well, now that we're all here, let's get going," Lexa said brightly.

She started to weave through the crowd with her bags. Only then did the dozens of people around the fountain snap to and start to move, as if Lexa's position as leader was universally acknowledged. Ariana fell into step with her as they started across campus, and the other girls formed a group around them. Ariana wondered where Palmer was. Her skin tingled pleasantly at the thought of him out there somewhere in the dark, possibly watching her.

And he might not be the only one watching. Ever since Lexa had spilled the beans about the secret societies on the APH campus, Ariana had constantly felt as if she were under some giant microscope, and now that she was going to be living in Privilege House, she felt it more than ever. She was sure that sometime soon, the society would be tapping new members, and Ariana was determined to be one of them—determined to conduct herself in a manner befitting Team Gold's ultra-exclusive society. Unfortunately, she wasn't entirely certain what the society was looking for, but she did know that Lexa Greene was a member.

"So . . . how are you?" Ariana asked Lexa as they walked side by side along the cobblestone path. By this point, news of Palmer and Lexa's breakup had traveled throughout the student body. All around them the campus's old-fashioned street lamps were ablaze, lighting the way toward the hill and Wolcott Hall beyond.

"Fine. I'll be fine," Lexa said gamely. "Everyone breaks up eventually, right?"

It was a line, obviously. She had broken up with the guy she loved less than three hours ago. But Ariana understood the need to keep up appearances. As they passed under one of the flickering lamps, Ariana noticed that beneath her dark bangs, Lexa's pretty, pert face was free of makeup. There was no evidence in her blue eyes that she had been crying, but her smile was slightly strained. Ariana felt a fleeting trace of guilt, having been the immediate cause of the breakup between Lexa and Palmer, but she let it go. Obviously there had been trouble brewing between the two of them for a while. Otherwise Palmer never would have developed feelings for Ariana in the first place. It wasn't entirely her fault that her friend was heartbroken.

"I'm just excited to move in," Lexa added, changing the subject. "You know we get to pick our own rooms, right?"

"Actually, I didn't know that," Ariana said.

"Guys are in Alpha tower, girls are in Bella," Maria explained.

"It's really A-tower and B-tower, but they have nicknames," Soomie explained, rolling her eyes as if the whole thing was just so juvenile. "Alpha for the alpha males, Bella for the supposedly *softer* gender," she said pointedly.

"So clever," Ariana said facetiously.

"Whatever you do, just don't pick 2B," Brigit cautioned. "Steer clear of that one."

"Why? What's with 2B?" Kaitlynn asked, glancing over her shoulder at Brigit.

"It's cursed," Brigit said with total seriousness.

The other girls laughed. "It's not cursed," Lexa said. "A girl died there back in the nineties and ever since then no one has wanted to live in 2B."

"Died? How?" Ariana asked.

"She killed herself," Maria said flatly. "With a carving knife she stole from the dining hall."

"Apparently she had some . . . issues," Soomie added.

"Ew. Omigod," Kaitlynn said, hand to her chest. "That's so awful! Okay, I am definitely not picking that room."

Ariana wanted to laugh. Kaitlynn grossed out by a little suicide? She'd killed a man, shooting him point-blank with a handgun. A man she supposedly loved. She so wished she could tell her friends about that tidbit from "Lily's" past. But then, Kaitlynn would expose Ariana's secrets, her own . . . indiscretions. And that, she could not have.

"Don't worry. We usually just use it as an extra closet," Lexa told them as they emerged from the circle of lesser dorms and headed up the steep incline toward Wolcott. The building's two towers of dorm rooms flanked a low-lying common area with floor-to-ceiling windows at the center that overlooked the campus on one side and the

Potomac River on the other. Ariana had been dying to see the inside of the exclusive building for days.

"Hey Ana, have you found a roommate yet?" Lexa asked. "Because Lily is solo if you two want to hook up."

"Omigosh, please say you're still solo," Kaitlynn said brightly, rushing forward a few steps to join them. "I would love it if we could room together."

Ariana felt the sudden urge to chew her own arm off. "We get to pick our own roommates, too?" she asked, stalling.

"Just one of the many perks of living in Privilege House," Soomie said, brushing one of her thick braids over her shoulder.

"And we're already paired off, so you two might as well pair off too," Maria suggested. "Before you get stuck with some loser like Tahira."

"Now, now," Lexa scolded with a laugh.

"What do you think, Ana? We can help each other figure this place out," Kaitlynn suggested, putting on a perfect, eager puppy dog act. Making it impossible for Ariana to turn her down without looking like a bitch in front of her friends.

"Sure. Sounds great," Ariana said, gritting her teeth.

Kaitlynn smiled in triumph. As the girls made their way up the hill at the front of the long line of students, Kaitlynn leaned toward Ariana's ear.

"It'll be just like old times," she whispered.

Right. Except back then I didn't know you were a psychotic, cold-blooded murderer.

Ariana felt so heavy with dread and defeat, her steps started to slow. Soon she was watching all four of her new friends from behind as they trotted up the hill, gabbing merrily with her sworn enemy. The enemy who was going to be sleeping in the next bed for the rest of the year.

CHOOSE

As Ariana walked into Wolcott Hall, she managed to let all her venomous feelings toward Kaitlynn go so that she could properly survey the rewards of her triumph. She was not disappointed.

The floor-to-ceiling windows Ariana had noticed from outside bordered the common study area, which was dotted with deep velvet couches and chairs. Dark maple study carrels, each with a wing-backed executive chair, had Internet hookups for the students' laptops. Off the study area on the east side, facing the river, was a small café with a coffee bar, pastry counter, and sandwich board, which opened onto a private patio. Next to that was a game room, complete with a pool table, several chess tables, and two flat-screen TVs with Wiis attached. Off the west side of the study area was a state-of-the art gym, packed with cardio machines, weight machines, yoga mats, exercise balls, and free weights.

"Wow. Definitely a step up from the Brenda T.," Kaitlynn said under her breath.

Ignoring her, Ariana walked over to two heavy double doors opposite the gym. "What's in here?" she asked, standing on her toes to try to see through the high windows.

"That's the theater," Lexa explained, yanking open the doors. She stepped over the threshold and flipped on the lights. Inside were at least twenty-five stadium-style seats with cup holders and fat armrests, facing a small movie screen. "It was donated by Vera Cassidy a few years ago. She's an alum."

"Vera Cassidy . . ." Ariana said, racking her brain. The name was familiar, but she couldn't place why.

"The director?" Soomie prompted, as if Ariana were somehow deficient for not knowing this. "First female auteur ever to win best director at the Independent Spirit Awards and the Oscars in the same year?"

"She makes sure we get first-run films up here," Maria said. "Guess she really liked this place."

"I can see why," Kaitlynn said, looking around the common area in a proprietary way that made Ariana's skin crawl.

"Come on, we'd better get upstairs and pick our rooms," Brigit said as the crowd outside the elevators started to grow.

"Like anyone's gonna take *our* rooms," Maria said.

"Don't rain on her parade. She's just excited," Soomie replied.

Just as they were about to approach the group of chatting girls outside the Bella tower elevators, a group of loud, raucous boys walked into the common area from Alpha tower. Ariana's heart tripped when she heard Palmer's uninhibited laugh. His heather gray APH T-shirt

was untucked over well-worn jeans, his black hair covered by a bat-
tered New York Yankees baseball cap. Ariana automatically glanced at
Lexa, who had gone pale beneath her smattering of adorable freckles.
Palmer and his crew, including Landon, Adam, Christian, and Rob,
paused when they saw the girls. Palmer's boyish grin faltered, but
not so much that a casual observer would notice. There was a brief
moment of uncomfortable silence, during which Palmer glanced at
Ariana in a way that made her knees puddle.

You're all mine now, she thought. *You're mine and I'm yours.* Happy
little goose bumps bubbled up all over her skin.

"Privilege House, baby!" Christian shouted, breaking the silence.

"Whooo!" Landon cheered, bending at the knees and leaning his
head back like a howling wolf. His long bangs fell backward from his
face, and the tendons on his skinny forearms stuck out as he clenched
his fists.

Maria and Soomie laughed as the two groups came together, hugging, jostling, and talking over one another. Brigit made a beeline
for Adam, whose tall frame towered over her, and the two of them
blushed while they spoke, just like they'd been doing all week. Even
Tahira and Allison rushed to join them, focusing their celebration on
Tahira's boyfriend, Rob, and the guys, of course. Lexa, however, didn't
move. Palmer slowly made his way over to Ariana and Lexa, his hands
in his pockets. Ariana wasn't sure if Lexa was making him come to
her—which would have been very cool of her—or if she was frozen by
her fear and emotion, which would have been decidedly less cool.

"Hey Ana," Palmer said with a small smile. Suddenly Ariana loved her new name. The way he said it made it the most beautiful word in the English language. "Lexa," he added, glancing at her. "Well, this is . . . awkward," he said with a sheepish smile, trying to lighten the mood.

"It shouldn't be," Lexa said casually, shrugging one shoulder. "We've always been friends, Palmer. There's no reason we can't still be."

Palmer raised his eyebrows, clearly surprised. "All right, then. Friends it is."

"Good," Lexa said.

"Good," Palmer echoed. He looked at Ariana with a glint in his eye and it was all she could do to keep a pleased blush from rising to her face. "Well, I guess I'll be seeing you ladies around."

"Later," Lexa said.

"'Bye," Ariana added.

Palmer rejoined his friends and Ariana turned to Lexa. "That went well. I'm impressed."

Lexa's hand shot out and gripped Ariana's wrist.

"Bathroom," Lexa said through her teeth. "Now."

As soon as they were through the swinging door next to the café, it opened again. Ariana fully expected to see Kaitlynn, horning in where she didn't belong, but instead Brigit came bounding through, all friendly concern.

"What happened?" Brigit asked.

"I can't do this." Lexa backed up against the marble counter of the sinks, pressing her palms against the edge. Tears shone in her eyes and her long, dark bangs got caught in her thick lashes as she attempted to blink them back. Her nose was rapidly turning red. Apparently the casual thing in the common room had been nothing but a very convincing act. "How am I supposed to live in the same dorm with him?"

Ariana's heart filled with a sour feeling that was part regret, part sympathy, and part annoyance. So Lexa wasn't over Palmer. Not at all. How was Ariana supposed to start dating the guy if the person she had chosen to be her best friend was busy moaning and groaning over him?

"It's gonna be okay, Lex," Brigit said, reaching for her arm.

Focus, Ariana. It isn't about you right now.

Right now it was about Lexa. If she and Lexa ever *were* going to be best friends, she had to start acting the part.

"It's true," Ariana said, handing Lexa a tissue from the marble counter. "It doesn't seem like it now, but you're going to get through this."

"No. I'm not." Lexa was wide-eyed. A single tear sluiced down her cheek. She wiped it away. "We had all these plans. . . . We were going to spend Christmas in Paris with my parents, spring break volunteering in the Dominican Republic. And what about the Crystal Ball in December? And the spring formal? We were supposed to go together. I had it all planned out."

"So you'll go with someone else," Ariana said decisively. "Someone better."

"Who's better?" Lexa blurted.

Ariana didn't have an answer for that question. For her, there was no one else.

"I mean . . . did *he* find someone better?" Lexa asked, pacing toward the bathroom stalls. "Is that what this is about? Did he meet someone over the summer?" She glanced at Ariana, and for a split second, Ariana was sure she was going to accuse her of stealing him out from under her peep-toes. "You were hanging out with him that first night. Did he mention anything? Any*one*?"

"No," Ariana said truthfully. He hadn't, in fact, even mentioned Lexa while he'd been flirting with Ariana.

"Then I don't get it," Lexa said, throwing up her hands. "I thought everything was fine."

"What did he say when he broke up with you?" Brigit asked. "Did he give you a reason?"

"No." Lexa shook her head and shrugged. "That's just it. Not a good one anyway. He said something about the two of us growing apart. He definitely didn't seem that distant the other night when we sneaked down to the boathouse together."

Ariana tasted bile in the back of her throat.

"I can't believe all the things I said to him." Lexa sniffled and looked up at the ceiling. "How much I missed him and how I couldn't wait to see him . . ." She started to cry in earnest. "I feel so stupid."

Ariana's heart went out to Lexa as a pair of sexy, teasing blue eyes flitted through her mind. She knew how it felt to be intimate with a guy one night and be completely dropped by him the next. To have your heart torn out. And Lexa was feeling that way now. It didn't matter that the boy who had hurt her was the boy Ariana wanted. What mattered was that her friend was in pain.

Maybe she could help. Maybe, if she played it right, she could help heal Lexa's broken heart, help her forget about the guy who'd hurt her. Which would mean she wouldn't care when Palmer moved on to someone else—namely, Ariana.

"Don't feel stupid, Lexa," Ariana said in a soothing voice. "If anything, he's the idiot. You don't need to be with a guy who doesn't appreciate you."

"She's right, Lexa. Boys suck," Brigit said, pulling Lexa into a hug.

Lexa pressed her face into Brigit's shoulder, wrapping her arms around her back. "They so do."

Ariana placed her hand on Lexa's back and moved it around in what she hoped was a comforting way.

"Don't worry. We're here for you," Ariana said. "We'll help you avoid him or trash his room or hook up with his best friend or do whatever it is you want to do to get back at him."

Lexa laughed. She turned her face so that she could see Ariana. "*There's* the Briana Leigh I know and love."

Ariana blinked. She wasn't quite sure how to take that. "What do you mean?"

"Nothing . . . just . . . back when we were little you were always the instigator. The plots, the pranks, the raiding the boys' dorms," Lexa said, grabbing another tissue and giving her nose a quick wipe. "I don't know. You just seem . . . different. Less . . . crazy. Not that that's a bad thing," she added quickly. "It's just something I noticed."

Ariana's whole body tensed. Damn that Briana Leigh and her over-the-top personality. And damn Lexa for being here and knowing that

Briana Leigh *had* that personality. If Lexa hadn't been at APH, Ariana could have just been herself and no one would have known the difference.

"I guess that's what losing both parents will do to you," Ariana said in a flat voice, going for the guilt, figuring it would change the subject.

"Your parents are both . . . ?" Brigit's eyes were wide with pity. Ariana looked away.

"Omigod, I'm so sorry. I'd heard about that, but I . . ." Lexa trailed off. "I'm such an idiot. Forget I said anything."

"It's fine." Ariana gave her a small smile as Lexa took a deep breath and moved to the sink to splash her face with water. Her fingers were balled into fists, which she quickly released. "I guess I could loosen up some."

But how the hell was she supposed to do that when she was in love with a guy who basically belonged to Lexa? When she was living in the same room as a manipulative, murderous wench? Before Ariana knew it, her fingernails were digging into her forearm.

"Ana? You okay?" Lexa asked, glancing at Ariana's arm in the mirror.

Ariana cleared her throat and quickly tucked her arms behind her back. "I'm fine," she said. "Loosening up even as we speak."

Liar. But you'd better figure out a way to chill, Ariana, she told herself. *Before Lexa starts to get suspicious.*

PERKS

Kaitlynn laughed in her sleep. It was one of the quirks Ariana used to find endearing about her. Precious. Now, as Ariana sat on the edge of her bed in her flimsy, white eyelet nightie, her bare feet flat on the glossy wood-paneled floor, the short laughs and occasional giggles made her tiny arm hairs stand on end. What was the girl dreaming about? What made a conniving, scheming psychopath laugh in her sleep?

Ariana sighed. All she wanted was a normal life. A second chance. To be free of her past and all the mistakes she had made. Free of all the people who had tried to stifle her and tell her what she could and could not have. But Kaitlynn was not going to let that happen. She was going to be here in this dorm room every day making damn sure Ariana was never able to put these things behind her. Never able to move on.

Suddenly, Kaitlynn turned over onto her side, her back now facing

Ariana. A quick sizzle of possibility raced through Ariana's veins. Her fingers reached for the feather pillow at the head of her bed. She had tried to do it once before and failed, but this opportunity was so much more convenient. Kaitlynn was dead asleep, mere footsteps away. All Ariana had to do was bring the pillow down over her face and hold it there. A minute or two of struggle and this could all be over. She could be free.

Her fingernails dug into the five-hundred-thread-count pillow case. Her jaw clenched.

Just do it, Ariana. She deserves it. She deserves it for everything she's done to you. Everything she did to Briana Leigh.

Briana Leigh.

Kaitlynn laughed again, and Ariana's grip loosened. She couldn't kill Kaitlynn. Obviously. If "Lillian Oswald" turned up dead, there would be an investigation. It would take the authorities about two seconds to discover that Lillian did not exist. Another two to run Kaitlynn's face through some database and learn who she really was. Two seconds more for them to turn to the roommate and discover her true identity as well.

And then it would all come to light. How Ariana had faked her own death. How she had murdered Briana Leigh Covington and sunk her to the bottom of Lake Page for the authorities to find in her place. How she'd assumed Briana Leigh's identity so she could attend APH. Ariana would be back at the Brenda T. before she could say "guilty as charged."

Ariana sighed. She placed her pillow back where it belonged and looked around the broad expanse of her dorm room. There were only four rooms on the top floor of Bella, each with a stunning view out its plate glass windows. Ariana and Kaitlynn's looked out over the campus and the thick green trees surrounding it. Their private suite consisted of a large bedroom, a bathroom, and a lounge area. The bedroom was outfitted with two dressers, two desks, and two walk-in closets. The bathroom boasted both a sunken tub and stall shower, and connected to the quaint lounge on the other side, which contained several bookshelves, a pullout couch, and a small flat-screen television. Each of the other three suites was exactly the same, except that Lexa and Maria had a bay window with a window seat and an unparalleled view of the river. Soomie and Brigit had chosen the room that looked north toward Washington D.C., and Tahira and Allison, Ariana's former roommate, were on the south side, facing the playing fields and gymnasium.

At least Ariana had snagged a better view than those two. Allison had been her roommate at Cornwall Hall during Welcome Week and a bitch to Ariana from day one. When it came to Tahira, Ariana had decided she didn't like the exhibitionist girl the moment she'd met her. The girl was everything Ariana detested—loud, conceited, brash, and braggy. But if Ariana had to live across the hall from her, at least she could take comfort in the fact that she'd be living in a superior room.

Kaitlynn rolled over onto her back and snorted. Ariana's lip curled in disgust. Her fingers curled into tight fists. She had to get out of there before she snapped and *did* kill the girl. She pushed her feet into her cashmere slippers and padded out into the hallway. At the center of the tower was a common-area bathroom, probably built in case the girls didn't want to invite visitors to use their own. Ariana shoved through the door and flipped the light switch. The fluorescents overhead blinked and crackled to life, winking in and out until they finally settled on a weak yellow glow. Apparently this room wasn't used very often. With its cracked ceramic tile and plain white walls, it looked as if it hadn't been renovated in twenty years, unlike the rest of Wolcott, which was updated, freshly painted, and pristine.

Ariana walked to the nearest mirror. She took a good look at herself in the dim half-light and saw the fear reflected in her ice blue eyes. The uncertainty.

"You can't let her do this to you," Ariana said to herself. Her voice was quiet but firm. She stared into her own eyes and forced the fear out. "You've worked too hard. This is your life. *Your* life. She can't have a piece of it. You can't let her."

Ariana heard the sound of door hinges squeaking. Her heart vaulted into her throat and she whirled around. There was a creak out in the hall. The unmistakable sound of careful, tiptoeing steps.

Kaitlynn?

The fluorescent lights buzzed and started to wink in and out again. Ariana cursed under her breath. If Kaitlynn was going to stage a sneak attack, she had to be ready. She looked around the unfamiliar room for a weapon, but there was nothing that wasn't nailed down. Soap dispenser, hand dryer, mirror. All bolted to the walls. The footsteps were getting closer. Ariana's eyes fell on the silver garbage can next to the sinks. She was just stooping to pick it up, when the door to the bathroom swung wide.

"There you are," Palmer whispered.

Ariana glanced up at him over her shoulder. She realized in a rush how she must look, half stooped over in her short nightgown, one hand tipping back the base of a refuse container.

"I just checked your room and your bed was empty, so I . . ." He paused and squinted at her. "What're you doing?"

It was a fair question.

"I . . . um . . . I thought I saw a scrap of tissue sticking out from under the can and I was going to throw it away, but I guess it's just these awful lights playing tricks on me." She carefully replaced the garbage can and stood up. Her fingers felt grimy, so she washed them quickly in the sink, taking a moment to breathe and let her adrenaline subside.

"So . . . I heard you and Lexa broke up," she said, glancing at Palmer in the mirror.

"Yeah." He stepped closer to her from behind.

His black hair was mussed and product free. He wore a pair of blue oversize cotton shorts with a white running stripe down the side and a wrinkled white T-shirt. His feet were entirely bare. Ariana's skin tingled as she realized he'd sneaked out of bed and risked getting caught, just for her.

"So . . . what're you doing here?" she asked.

Palmer smirked. They both knew exactly what he was doing here. Ariana thought of Lexa. Of how Lexa would have killed for Palmer to

have made the same effort for her. She felt sorry for the girl and exhilarated to have been chosen over her, all at the same time. Then Palmer
closed in and ran his hands down the lengths of her bare arms.

Ariana's heart stopped beating. Screw Lexa. She and Palmer were
half-dressed and alone in the middle of the night in an obviously
unused room. What Lexa didn't know wouldn't hurt her. Ariana turned
around and her hip bones met his. Without hesitation he pulled her
into a deep, passionate, searching kiss. Ariana's hands were wet but
she buried them in his hair anyway. He pressed her back against the
cold ceramic sink, kissing her more and more deeply until her back
was arched so far she had to brace her hands on the sink behind her
to keep from falling.

Finally he pulled back. His eyes searched hers as if desperate to
memorize them. "I've been wanting to do that all night."

Ariana's lips hummed. "Glad you finally did."

Palmer took her hand lightly in his and tugged her toward a small
wooden bench near the door. He sat down and pulled her onto his
lap sideways, looping his arms casually around her waist, as if this
was something they did every day. The familiarity of the gesture
made Ariana's heart swell. It was as if they were already an established
couple.

"So, what do you think of Privilege House?" he asked with a
smirk.

"If this is one of the perks, I like it," she replied.

"Thanks for talking me into keeping my mouth shut earlier,"
Palmer said, running his hand up and down her thigh. "I don't think

I could have handled it if the blue team had ended up living here. I might have had to punch something."

Ariana smiled. She had helped him. He appreciated her. "You're welcome," she said.

He reached his hand around the back of her neck and pulled her lips to his for another kiss. Before long, sitting sidesaddle across his legs became quite uncomfortable, and Ariana maneuvered around until she was straddling his waist, her knees pressing awkwardly into the hard bench. He tried to adjust himself, to pull her even closer, but her knee banged into the wall behind him. She let out a quiet yelp as pain radiated through her leg.

"Sorry." He was breathless, flushed. "Maybe we should take this into the lounge."

The lounge. There were couches and chairs down there. It would have been much more comfortable. But it was also an open common area. An area in which they could easily be stumbled upon by one of her floormates. By Lexa.

Suddenly, Ariana's chest flooded with guilt.

"No."

She pushed away from him and scrambled to her feet. Her night-gown had become completely twisted around her body and she quickly adjusted it so the white cotton loosened from her skin. As Palmer looked her up and down, she wondered exactly how see-through the garment was.

"No?" Palmer raised his brows, surprised.

"I'm sorry. I have to go," Ariana said as she whipped the door open. She paused on the threshold and looked back at him. His confusion and disappointment were so adorable she almost went back. But she couldn't do that to Lexa. Couldn't do this at all. Not until she figured out what the wisest move would be.

"But thanks for stopping by," she said with a small smile.

Then she walked back to her room, where she was absolutely certain of a night with zero sleep.

THE CRAZIEST

"I have to miss the first few mornings of classes so I can take their stupid entrance exams," Kaitlynn said as she touched up her lip gloss, leaning in toward the mirror above her dresser on Tuesday morning. "Any tips?"

Ariana said nothing. Slowly, deliberately, she buttoned up the front of her white oxford shirt and tucked it into the waistband of her blue and gray plaid skirt. Then she slipped a gray tie around her collar and went to work on the knot, standing in front of the full-length mirror on the back of the door. She had awoken after a surprisingly good night's sleep to bright sunshine streaming through her huge window. An overwhelming sense of well-being had washed over her. A feeling that somehow, some way, everything was going to be all right. That eventually she would find a way to fix the Kaitlynn situation, find a way to have Palmer as her boyfriend *and* Lexa as her best friend. Find a way to get everything she wanted. Ariana had always taken care of herself. She just had to have a touch of patience. Everything was going to work out in the end, just as it always did. Starting with making today great.

Accordingly, Ariana's plan was to pretend Kaitlynn did not exist. If the girl did not exist, then she couldn't ruin her good mood.

"Ariana? Hello? I asked you a question," Kaitlynn said, turning around.

Ariana gritted her teeth over the use of her real name. She wanted to correct the girl, but that would mean acknowledging her existence. Instead, she finished knotting her tie and selected a pair of socks from her dresser. She sat down on the edge of her bed and shimmied a sock over her foot.

"The silent treatment? That's mature," Kaitlynn said with a laugh, shoving the lip gloss wand back into its tube. She grabbed her leather messenger bag and slung it over her shoulder. "Then I guess you're not going to tell me where you disappeared to in the middle of the night."

Ariana's eyes automatically flicked up. How had Kaitlynn known she was gone? Had Palmer woken her up when he'd opened the door? Had Kaitlynn seen him? How much did she know? Oh God. Would she tell Lexa?

Every muscle in Ariana's body tensed. So much for not letting Kaitlynn get to her.

"I'm always watching, Ariana," Kaitlynn said, as if reading Ariana's mind. She glanced in the mirror one last time, fluffed her short hair, then opened the door and flounced out. "Wish me luck!"

The door slammed and Ariana threw one of her loafers at it, letting out a growl of frustration. The sound was still hanging in the air when the door opened again and Ariana heard Lexa, Maria, Soomie, and Brigit shouting hellos and good-mornings to Kaitlynn. The door pushed the shoe aside and Ariana jumped up to grab it as her friends filed in. While her back was to them, Ariana cursed the school's policy of lockless doors in the dorm rooms—a policy she'd appreciated the first week of school when she was going around stealing people's things so she could pay off Kaitlynn. But right then, she could have used a moment to compose herself before her friends walked in. She took a deep breath to calm her rattled nerves. Kaitlynn did not exist. She did not exist.

God, how she wished the girl did not exist.

"Good morning," Ariana said, walking back to her bed in one sock. She shoved her foot into the shoe as she dropped down onto her mattress again. "Everyone ready for the first day of class?"

"Ugh. You're a morning person," Maria said, dropping flat on her back atop Kaitlynn's bed. Her uniform was, as always, wrinkled, untucked, and messy—a button undone here, a hem falling there.

"Ignore her. She's only had one espresso so far this morning," Lexa joked, perching on Ariana's desk chair. Lexa's light blue shirt was formfitting, her pleated skirt slightly longer than everyone else's. She wore argyle socks pulled up to her knees and black lace-up shoes with a slight heel. With her expertly applied makeup and shiny dark hair loose down her back, she could have been the cover girl for the APH catalogue. Ariana was pleased to find her so well put together. On the morning after a breakup, most girls rocked the *I'm too depressed to groom* look. Did this mean that Lexa was getting over Palmer already?

"I love that we have a café in the building, but their espresso is subpar," Maria said, closing her eyes and crooking her arm over her forehead.

"Dining hall, then?" Ariana asked, quickly slipping on her second shoe.

"Yes. But first, we have to talk to you about the NoBash," Brigit said, walking over to the window and leaning back against the slight ledge. Her dozens of colorful plastic bracelets tumbled down her arm and came to rest just above her hand.

"The what now?" Ariana asked. She opened her satchel to make sure she had everything she needed. *Laptop, check. Notebook, check. Pens, check.*

"The NoBash," Soomie said, checking her BlackBerry before slipping it back into the outer pocket of her suede bag. "It's this hugely important event held at the Norwegian Embassy every year."

"Dignitaries from around the world, crazy paparazzi, high-security metal detectors ever since that dude from Brazil managed to sneak in that scary collapsible sword thingy," Maria said, waving her hand around. "Blah, blah, blah."

"Don't scare her!" Lexa scolded. "It's an incredibly fabulous party," she assured Ariana.

"And you need to know about it because A) Brigit's family throws it, B) everyone here is dying to go, and C) not everyone gets to," Soomie added.

Ariana's shoulders tensed. *Not everyone gets to go?* Were they here to warn her that she wasn't going to be invited to this exclusive party?

"My parents only give me a handful of invites," Brigit said. Her parents were king and queen of Norway, which made Brigit a genuine princess. Not that she looked, dressed, or acted like one.

"And she distributes them in a very discerning fashion," Lexa added, checking her nails.

"So if you see people kissing up to me in the next few days, that's why," Brigit put in with a mock-haughty look, which her easy grin quickly erased.

So . . . they were here to tell her she had to start kissing Brigit's butt. Ariana wasn't sure whether to be offended by the suggestion or grateful for the warning. She said a silent thank-you that Kaitlynn wasn't around to hear all of this.

"Wow. Such power," Ariana said.

"I know. Isn't it cool?" Brigit replied with a laugh. "Of course I've already reserved one for you."

Ariana's heart actually fluttered in excitement. So this wasn't about making her jump through hoops. She'd already become so integral to the group that Brigit had decided to include her. She had really come a long way in the past week.

"Thanks," she said with a smile.

"Delivery for Ms. Al Mahmood."

Ariana and her friends all turned toward the open door. A young woman in a pencil skirt was handing a big pink-and-purple-striped box over to Tahira in her room across the hallway.

"Who's that?" Ariana asked.

"Our concierge," Lexa replied. "Each tower has one. She signs for our packages, makes sure we get our laundry on time, orders food for us. Stuff like that."

Damn. Why, why, why couldn't she call Billings and show off?

"Sweet! It's a care package from Lissa!" Tahira cooed, checking the card. "Lissa Braverman?" she said to the girls across the hall, her expression cocky. "We did Monte Carlo together last March."

"Congratulations, T. Everyone wants to be the girl who gets to hold Lissa Braverman's hair back over the toilet bowl," Maria said sarcastically, without even opening her eyes.

Brigit, Soomie, and Ariana laughed, while Lexa merely smirked, her back to Tahira. Lissa Braverman was a well-known socialite, international nightclub heiress, and total lush. Back when Ariana was a junior at Easton, her friend Paige Ryan used to hang out with Lissa's older sister Mischa. Even then Mischa used to complain about her sister the wild child, so it was no surprise to Ariana to see what Lissa had become. Tahira shot them all a look of death and slammed the door to her room.

"God," Brigit spat. "I can't believe I have to invite her."

"She gets to go to the NoBash?" Ariana asked, surprised. Brigit and Tahira hated each other.

"Her *and* Zuri," Soomie replied. "Their parents are international players, so the king and queen insist Brigit invite them."

"Fab," Ariana said flatly.

"They're not *that* bad," Lexa put in.

"Whatevs. Tahira is always trying to outdo me, especially at the NoBash since she knows how important it is to my family, so it's very important that my friends and I are the most fabulous people at the party," Brigit said, suddenly flipping into no-nonsense mode. "I'm going to need you guys to bring your gowns by my room for approval, and no one is allowed to wear purple. I've got dibs on purple."

Ariana nodded, impressed by Brigit's take-charge attitude. Soomie whipped out her BlackBerry and made a note of Brigit's demands.

"Got that, Maria?" she asked, slipping the PDA away again.

"Lexa will remind me," Maria said lazily.

"And Ana, you and Lily have to keep your eyes on Tahira," Brigit said. Ariana bristled at the mention of Kaitlynn—at her inclusion in the conversation and the group.

"We do?" Ariana asked.

"You live right across the hall from her, so you have to be my eyes and ears," Brigit said, stepping away from the window. "You guys need to find out what she and Allison are wearing, who they're bringing, what jewelry they're borrowing from which jeweler. If Tahira so much as makes a call to her stylist, I need to know about it. Okay?"

"Absolutely," Ariana said. Tahira was also a princess of sorts, the daughter of the ruler of Dubai. Their friends had dubbed the rivalry between the girls "the Princess Wars," and they all seemed to find the whole thing highly amusing, even though it was deadly serious to Brigit and Tahira.

"And make sure you tell Lily," Brigit added.

"I will, but I don't know if she'll be up for it," Ariana said, keeping her tone casual. "I think she and Tahira have kind of bonded."

This was a total lie. As far as she knew Kaitlynn and Tahira had done nothing more than introduce themselves. But it couldn't hurt to plant the seed that Kaitlynn was aligning herself with Brigit's enemy. Even if Lexa did keep insisting that Tahira had her good qualities. Ariana had yet to see any, and the other girls seemed to be blind to them as well.

"Really? Why?" Soomie said, wrinkling her nose, as if the very idea of conversing with Tahira was noxious.

Ariana did her best not to smile. "I have no idea."

"Okay, well then, it's up to you, Ana," Brigit said.

"Well, we already know Tahira's bringing Robbie," Maria said, pulling some stray hair in front of her face to check for split ends. "You should definitely be able to snag someone better than him."

Brigit winced. "I hate the date part. Sometimes I wish we still lived in the days when it was unacceptable for girls to ask out boys. Let them be the ones who have to get all nervous and sweaty all the time."

"Why don't you ask Adam?" Ariana suggested.

Brigit blushed as Maria lifted her head for the first time. "You and Scholarship Boy? It's like a fairy tale."

"He's . . . nice," Brigit said, fiddling with the fringe on one of Ariana's pillows and avoiding eye contact. "I don't know . . . we'll see. All I know is I don't want to be dateless. Dateless is bad."

"I'm right there with you, Brigit," Lexa said, staring straight ahead at nothing. "I was supposed to bring Palmer, but . . ."

Ariana glanced at Maria and Soomie. Downward spiral time.

"Screw Palmer," Maria said, sitting up. "It'll be fun, just us girls."

"Yeah. Who needs him?" Soomie said.

"I think maybe I do," Lexa said, her bottom lip quivering.

"Oh, Lex! It's gonna be okay." Brigit walked over and wrapped her arms around Lexa's shoulders as a few tears leaked down the dark-haired girl's cheeks. Ariana and the others gathered around her as well, all encouraging words and sympathetic nothings. Lexa's tears were just starting to subside when a shriek sounded from across the hall.

"Peanut brittle!? What was that bitch thinking? She *knows* I'm allergic!" Tahira screamed. Her door opened and she flung a tin across the hallway so hard Ariana had just enough time to duck out of the way before it took her ear off. "Get rid of it," Tahira shouted at Allison. "Dump the whole box!"

Allison stood there for a moment—tall, pale, and blond—hovering over Tahira's shorter, darker, curvier self. The girl was clearly dumbfounded by the fact that she was being screamed at and ordered around by her friend.

"Do it before I touch something that was contaminated by peanuts!" Tahira shrieked. "Unless you *want* me to die!"

Allison dutifully grabbed the box and scurried out, making for the stairwell like a panicked mouse.

"Ugh! What is wrong with people!?" Tahira shouted.

She slammed her door again, this time so hard the mirrors on Ariana's walls shook. For a long moment there was dead silence, then

Ariana and her friends cracked up laughing, relieving all the tension in the air.

"What was that?" Ariana asked, her hand to her chest.

Maria lazily pushed herself up on her elbows as if nothing unusual had happened. "That was Atherton-Pryce Hall's favorite drama queen being her dramatic self."

"She's deathly allergic to peanuts," Lexa said, smiling. Apparently the sideshow had distracted her from her pain for the moment. "She carries an EpiPen everywhere just in case."

"That's scary," Ariana said, wishing Kaitlynn had such a convenient Achilles' heel.

Soomie opened a compact mirror and handed it to Lexa. She ran her fingers over her eyeliner and brushed a tear from her chin. Then she slapped the mirror closed, took a deep breath, and shook her hair back.

"How do I look?" she asked, standing.

"Perfect," Ariana replied.

"Good. Let's go meet the guys for breakfast."

Ariana's heart sank. That was why Lexa looked so good. She knew she was going to see Palmer and she wanted to show him what he was missing. Ariana should have known. She had been looking forward to seeing Palmer herself, but now, not so much. Not if he was going to be gazing longingly at Lexa. Brigit pulled Maria up from Kaitlynn's mattress and they all started to gather their things.

"Lissa! No . . . no . . . I don't care how hungover you are, don't you dare hang up on me!" Tahira shouted from behind her closed door.

"You sent me peanuts!? Was this some kind of sadistic joke, or are you just that stupid!?"

"Wow. She's a little bit crazy, isn't she?" Ariana said, shouldering her bag.

"Oh, yeah," Soomie replied, "Craziest girl at APH."

Ariana glanced over at Kaitlynn's bed.

Not quite the *craziest.*

DISTRACTION

"Thanks for coming with. I just need one more shot and I'll be good," Maria said over her shoulder as she and Ariana walked into the Hill after breakfast. The dining hall waiter had cut Maria off after her third espresso, so she was in search of someone else to feed her habit.

"No problem," Ariana replied.

The junior/senior lounge was mostly deserted—everyone was rushing to get to their first classes of the year—but there were a couple of stragglers in line at the coffee counter. Ariana was about to follow Maria there when she spotted Palmer out of the corner of her eye, lounging on a brocaded couch, texting on his phone while sipping an iced tea. So this was where he'd been hiding. Everyone had felt his absence at the breakfast table, especially Lexa. But here he was, just a couple of doors away. Ariana loved that he was so laid-back about the first day that he was still chilling at the Hill five minutes before class was to start. He looked ridiculously handsome in his white oxford shirt, blue and gold striped tie, and blue blazer. Vivid memories from last night's encounter in the bathroom rushed in on her in full force. As if he could sense her presence, Palmer looked up, pocketed his phone, and approached. Ariana looked warily at Maria, but the girl was so intent on getting her espresso fix, she didn't even glance back to see where Ariana had gone.

"Good morning, lovely," Palmer said with a grin.

Ariana's insides shivered with pleasure. As nicknames went, that wasn't bad. "We missed you at breakfast."

"I ate in here," he said, leaning so close she could smell the fresh scent of his shampoo. He extracted the baseball he always kept in his pocket, tossed it up, and caught it. "I didn't feel like dealing with the drama this morning."

"Ah," Ariana said.

"So, I was thinking, want to have lunch together later?" he asked, his smile so inviting it was hardly possible to resist.

"I don't know, Palmer," Ariana said, keeping one eye on Maria, who was paying for her drink. "I think it's too soon."

Palmer took a sip of his iced tea and nodded. "Okay, but don't keep me waiting too long," he said with a leading grin. Then he lifted his eyebrows and walked out of the room backward. Ariana shook her head at him but couldn't help smiling. The second she did, he turned and jogged off. At that exact moment, Maria finished her transaction and turned around to look for Ariana. The timing couldn't have been more perfect. She hadn't seen a thing.

"What happened to you?" Maria asked.

"Nothing. Just figured I'd wait by the door," Ariana said as they started out the door. "So listen, I'm kind of worried about Lexa."

"I know," Maria said, taking a sip of her coffee. "I've never seen her like this. We were up all night going over and over and over it. I didn't tell her this, but it sounds to me like Palmer's just being boy-fickle. He's done. He's moved on. End of story. But she cannot stop analyzing every word he's ever said to her."

This did not sound promising.

"I think we need to do something to distract her," Ariana said, stepping into the sunlight. "To take her mind off of Palmer."

So I can finally have him all to myself, she added silently.

"Got any ideas?" Maria asked.

"Not yet, but I'll work on it," Ariana said. "It's too bad the NoBash is over a week away. I bet that's pretty distracting."

"Oh, it can be," Maria said with a small smile. She slipped on her aviator sunglasses as they started across campus.

"Are you going with Landon?" Ariana asked.

"Probably not," Maria said, looking ahead thoughtfully. "Too many paparazzi. If they got a shot of the two of us together, and my dad saw it . . ." She slashed her finger across her throat and let her tongue loll out the corner of her mouth.

Ariana laughed. "You mean boarding school in Europe."

"Death would be preferable," Maria said drily. "We go to a few events a year 'as friends,'" she said in a meaningful tone. "But I think Soomie's thinking about asking him."

"Whatever we do for Lexa, maybe we should do it for Soomie, too. Get her mind off Landon," Ariana suggested.

"Yeah, I think you're going to need to give her a lobotomy for that," Maria said.

Ariana laughed and together they climbed the stone steps to the class building. Inside, the air was cool and smelled of musty books, freshly waxed floors, and decades of knowledge. Students rushed up the stairs; a pair of teachers spoke in hushed tones outside an open classroom door; somewhere someone was writing on a whiteboard, the marker squeaking and squealing. Ariana grinned, all lit up from the inside.

"God, you're a *school* person, too, aren't you?" Maria said, rolling her eyes. "It's getting harder and harder to like you," she joked.

"Thanks a lot," Ariana said, her smile intact.

Maria laughed and paused outside a classroom. "This is me. We'll talk Mission: Distraction later."

"Definitely."

Ariana turned and started up the stairs. On the landing above, Kaitlynn was standing near the wall, talking to Tahira of all people. Ariana's heart skipped a nervous beat. She had completely made up that bit about the two of them hanging out. When had they gotten all chummy? And what, exactly, were they talking about?

"What's up, Love?" Ariana said to Tahira, not wanting either of them to think she was intimidated by their alliance.

"Too dim to make up your own insults, Briana Leigh?" Tahira asked, tossing her thick, dark mane over her shoulder. She had coined the name for Ariana the week before when she'd beaten her in tennis, but now that Ariana had beaten her back—winning a good deal of money from her in the process—she'd reassigned the name to Tahira.

"Just wanted to remind you who's the loser and who's the winner," Ariana teased, continuing up the stairs.

Kaitlynn said her good-byes to Tahira and quickly fell into step with Ariana. "What was that all about?" she asked.

"Oh, if you'd been here for welcome week, you'd know," Ariana replied blithely, wanting nothing more than to remind Kaitlynn that her position here was not as secure as her own. Maybe Ariana only had a week on the girl, but it was something.

"So you're talking to me again, then? Good," Kaitlynn said. "Because Tahira just filled me in on this NoBash thing and I'm intrigued."

"Goody for you," Ariana replied, scanning the numbers on the doors, looking for her French classroom. She had a feeling she knew what was coming.

"Yeah, it sounds like fun. So I guess you'll be getting me an invite then, right?" Kaitlynn said.

Sometimes Kaitlynn was just so predictable. Ariana sighed and stopped in front of room 212. "Can't you ever do anything for yourself? Or are you just too feeble?"

A flash of anger passed through Kaitlynn's eyes, then left as quickly as it had come. "Why bother doing things myself when I have you to do them for me?"

With that, she skipped down the steps and let the front door of the building slam behind her.

THE PLAN

"I trust everyone had a fine summer full of traveling, exploring, and general enlightenment," Mr. Halloran said, pacing the front of Ariana's honors English classroom later that morning. He was an older man with a gray beard and shaggy gray hair, who wore his tiny spectacles all the way down at the end of his nose. His tie was loosened, his houndstooth jacket new, his leather loafers scuffed and worn. He had decorated his classroom with huge glossy photographs of literary places he'd visited—the moors of England from *Wuthering Heights*, the Marabar caves from *A Passage to India*, the streets of Dublin from *Portrait of the Artist as a Young Man*. The photos alone were enough to endear him to Ariana. He was a cataloguer. Not to mention a bit of a showoff.

"And I trust you all had time to read through at least ten of the books on your summer reading lists, as required," he added. This was met with groans from the room. "So, I would like you to choose one of those books, turn to the person next to you, and spend the next forty minutes discussing that book with this person, delineating all its merits and flaws. Time starts . . . now."

Ariana was seated near the window. When she turned to face the person next to her, she found a handsome African-American boy with close-cropped hair and a friendly smile. She had spotted him moving into Privilege House the night before, but now that they were mere inches away, she could see that he was one of the more athletic boys on the APH campus. His biceps strained at the fabric of his blazer and his neck was so thick it was barely contained by his collar and tie. On his feet he wore a pair of expensive but mud-spattered running shoes. The mud was fresh, as if he'd just gone for a jog that morning.

"Hi," he said. "I'm Conrad Royce. My friends, unfortunately, call me Connie." He had a deep baritone voice that sent tremors through her chest. It was a sexy voice. The kind of voice that was perfect for poetry readings. The kind that could definitely carry a tune. "You were on Team Gold too, right? You were the cox in the crew race."

"Yeah, that was me. Ana Covington," she replied. "I'm a transfer and I have no idea what was on the summer reading list."

Conrad whipped a sheet of paper out of the binder on his desk. "Here you go."

He'd highlighted all the books he'd read. Ariana did a quick scan and estimated he'd read at least fifty of the hundred books listed. Far more than required. She decided she liked this Conrad Royce.

"Okay. I can discuss some of these. Which one do you want to do?" Ariana asked.

"I'll take on Hemingway. That guy seriously pisses me off," Conrad said, turning fully in his seat to face her.

Ariana laughed, then covered her mouth with her hand as Mr. Halloran turned a scolding eye on her.

"Why?" she asked

"I just don't understand why everyone thinks he's so great," Conrad said, placing his large palms on his knees. "I mean, I never know where his characters are, I get all turned around by the conversations and have to go back to figure out who's saying what. It's like, give me *something*. Some description, some emotion, some clarification. Anything. I need some meat in my literature. Paragraphs, even."

"Wow. I've never heard anyone bash Hemingway before," Ariana said.

"Sorry. I suppose you like him, huh? 'Oh, Brett and Jake were just made for each other,'" he joked, putting on a high-pitched voice and clasping his hands under his chin.

Ariana laughed again. "No. Actually, I hated *The Sun Also Rises*. I don't get why everyone is so in love with Jake. He's too flawed for my taste."

"You don't go for flaws in your heroes?" Conrad asked.

"I wouldn't say that, exactly. Of course they have to have *some* flaws . . . otherwise they have nowhere to go in the story, but that guy? What a loser," Ariana said.

Conrad laughed. "Tell me about it."

"But you also read *For Whom the Bell Tolls* and *A Farewell to Arms*,"

Ariana said, consulting his list. "Why keep going back if you hated it so much?"

"I figured I had to be missing something. Besides, just because you don't like something doesn't mean it's not important work, right?" he said. "Reading his stuff helped me understand the postwar world he was writing in, and it got me started on his contemporaries, too. F. Scott Fitzgerald and Gertrude Stein were pretty cool."

Ariana grinned. She was loving this. Intelligent discourse with a good-looking guy. Her heart tingled with excitement and she sat back in her chair slightly, filled with an overwhelming sense of satisfaction. This was where she was supposed to be. This was what she should have been doing for the last two years instead of listening to Crazy Cathy babble about her imaginary unicorn friend or watching Tracy the guard suck pumpkin seeds between her teeth or sitting through those excruciating sessions with Doctor Meloni. If only he could see her now. If only he knew that she'd gotten exactly what she wished for.

And also, Conrad was hot. If she hadn't already started something up with Palmer, she would have asked him to sit with her at lunch.

Suddenly, Ariana's phone vibrated. Startled, she glanced at Mr. Halloran, but he didn't seem to have heard. Ariana grappled in her bag for the phone. On the screen was a text from Lexa.

OMG this class SO boring. Will never make it thru this yr.
R U liking ur first day?

Ariana smiled, pleased that Lexa was checking in on her. She texted back quickly.

Actually having fun. C U @ lunch!

She sent the text and slipped her phone back into her bag. When she looked up at Conrad again, he smiled adorably.

"Getting texts during class, Miss Covington? For shame," he joked. "Who was it?"

"Lexa Greene. Do you know her?" Ariana asked.

"Lexa? Not well, but yeah. Everyone knows Lexa Greene." And then he blushed slightly, looking down at his notebook. Ariana's heart skipped a thousand beats.

That's it.

The easiest way to get over a guy was to find a better one. Why hadn't she thought of this before? Lexa had said it herself in the bathroom last night—*"Who's better?"* Well, why not Conrad Royce? He was intelligent. Definitely handsome. And a runner, just like Lexa. Plus that voice could melt steel, let alone a broken heart.

"So, Conrad, what did you do this summer?" she asked, leaning her chin on her hand. "Aside from all this reading? Anything interesting?"

As Conrad launched into the story of his summer learning the ins and outs of his family's winery business in Northern California, Ariana smiled to herself. She couldn't wait to tell Maria about the plan. If she had her way, Lexa would have a new boyfriend before the NoBash, and Ariana and Palmer would be free to be together.

FEAR

The homework list was brutal, but not half as brutal as the list of goals Ariana constructed for herself after the first day of classes was complete. Throughout the day she had come to realize that she was at a serious disadvantage. The instructors at Atherton-Pryce Hall were far more intense than most of those at Easton. Each of them had launched into lessons with gusto, presuming their students could simply pick up from where they'd left off the year before. Which, Ariana had learned with awe, all of them could. She, however, hadn't been inside a classroom in over two years, and as intelligent as she was, she couldn't remember every little fact she'd learned back at Easton. She had a lot of catching up to do.

Which was why she was the last person to leave the Jonathan Hayes Memorial Library that night. When she'd first arrived after dinner, the place had been humming with activity, computer screens glowing, book pages flipping, soda cans popping open. By the time she left—

just after ten o'clock—it was as quiet as a tomb, and the middle-aged librarian had been forced to roust her from her study carrel and usher her out through the darkened stacks.

"I'm so sorry," Ariana said as the woman held open the heavy oak door for her. "I had no idea it had gotten so late."

"It's all right, Miss Covington," the woman said with a genuine smile. "It's nice to see such dedication on the first day. I'm going to keep my eye on you. I have a feeling you're going to go far."

From your lips to God's ears, Ariana thought. It was one of her mother's favorite phrases, and her heart panged as she recalled the southern lilt of her mom's voice.

"Thanks," she said. "I'm sure I'll be seeing you tomorrow."

Ariana rushed down the steps to the cobblestone pathway that ran along the inner circle of campus. All the iron street lamps were aglow, and the benches and trees threw oddly shaped shadows across the grass. There wasn't another soul on the otherwise dark circle; the burbling fountain at the center of campus was the only source of sound. A breeze tickled the back of Ariana's neck and she felt an inexplicable finger of fear slide down her spine. She quickened her steps.

"Privilege House may have its perks, but it's definitely not conveniently located," she said aloud, hoping the sound of her own voice would soothe her nerves.

Suddenly, footsteps scuffled on the path behind her. Ariana's heart constricted as she whirled around, ready to face down Kaitlynn or Tahira or whoever else might be stalking her . . . but there was no one there. Another breeze tossed her long auburn hair back from her face. Ariana squinted into the relative darkness. Nothing. No moving shadows. Just the merrily bubbling fountain.

Ariana's phone beeped, scaring her heart into her throat. She whipped it out of her bag. There was a text from Lexa.

Where R U? De-stress dance party in our room stat!

Ariana took a breath. Lexa wanted to hang out. This was a good thing. She started walking again, a bit faster this time, telling herself she was simply late for a party. That was all. She wasn't in the least bit freaked by the—

Scuffle. Scuffle.

Arian's lungs tightened. She turned around again, this time walking even faster. She had taken two steps toward the outer circle of dorm buildings and the hill that towered beyond, when suddenly everything went dark.

Scuffle.

Ariana froze in her tracks. Every single light on campus had been extinguished. The street lamps, the office lights, the emergency lights over the doorways. She was surrounded by unrelenting darkness.

Blackout. It's just a blackout.

Another scuffle. Ariana took in a broken, terrified breath just as a coarse black bag was yanked over her face.

NEOPHYTES

"What's going on? Who are you? Where are you taking me?"

Ariana was terrified, but she was not going to let whoever these people were see that. She asked her questions calmly, rationally, even as her heart tried to jackhammer its way through her ribs. There were at least two assailants. They pinned her arms to her sides as they hurried her across campus. Completely blinded by the black bag over her head, Ariana tripped on one of the irregular cobblestones and flew forward. She heard someone, a male someone, curse under his breath as he righted her. Other than that, no one said a word.

They were headed north, in the opposite direction from Wolcott Hall. Ariana was almost sure of it. Were they going toward the chapel? Or the underclassman dorms? The parking lot?

She got her answer a second later when they stopped abruptly and a strong hand pushed down on the top of her head, forcing her to bend. She was shoved awkwardly forward and her head banged into someone else's as her knees hit the back of a leather seat.

"Ow! Watch it!"

Kaitlynn. Ariana's whole body started to shake with fear. Kaitlynn was in the car. Was she a part of this? If she was, Ariana was going to kill her. Screw the consequences.

"What the hell is going on?" Ariana demanded.

Someone shoved her backward so she was sitting on the seat properly.

"A—Ana?" Kaitlynn's voice replied. It was muffled, much like her own. "Is that you?"

Ariana bit down on her tongue. She couldn't decide if Kaitlynn was playing her, or if she seriously couldn't see her.

"What the hell is going on, *Lily*?" Ariana asked pointedly.

The car door slammed.

"I don't know," Kaitlynn whispered, cuddling close to Ariana's side. "I was just heading upstairs from the gym when someone threw a bag over my head and dragged me here. Whoever it was, I scratched the crap out of his arm, but I couldn't take him blindfolded."

Ariana stopped breathing. Both she and Kaitlynn were being kidnapped by faceless sentries? There was only one explanation.

"Game over," she muttered.

"What? What do you mean?" Kaitlynn whispered.

"It's the FBI, obviously," Ariana replied. "They found out where we were somehow and they're taking us back."

There was a moment of silence as Kaitlynn took this in. Outside the car, a few male voices spoke in low tones.

"No. Not possible. Why would they do it like this? Why not just come in with handcuffs and guns and all that crap?" Kaitlynn asked.

"Oh, I don't know, probably because this school is full of well-connected international billionaires," Ariana replied. "They probably want to keep it quiet. Cover it up so that all the congressmen and senators and kings and queens won't have to deal with everyone knowing their kids' high-security school was infiltrated by two escaped criminals," she said sarcastically.

One of the front doors opened and the car bounced as someone got in behind the wheel. Both Ariana and Kaitlynn fell silent, knowing better than to talk about anything until they knew exactly who they were dealing with. The car engine started, and they were off. Before long the car dipped off the paved road and bumped along some kind of rocky terrain. Suddenly, Ariana felt a hot, searing terror go through her. Were they taking her back to Lake Page? To the place where she'd murdered Briana Leigh and she and Kaitlynn had disposed of the body?

The drive couldn't have been more than fifteen minutes long, but it felt like an eternity to Ariana. When the car finally stopped, the driver did not get out. Instead, the doors on both sides of the backseat were flung open and a hand closed around Ariana's arm. It was small and feminine, but strong. The woman dragged Ariana out of the backseat and onto an uneven, pockmarked dirt path. Ariana tripped along, still unable to see, and wondered if the United States government was secretly running firing squads in rural Virginia.

"Stop."

Ariana froze. She heard a crackle and sensed a warmth on her right side. Was that a fire? The woman turned her so that she was facing the flames, then let her go. For a moment, Ariana couldn't process this information. Should she make a move for the bag over her head? Try to run? But then, out of nowhere, the bag was torn free. Ariana's relieved lungs filled with oxygen and the heady scent of burning wood. To her left, Kaitlynn whirled around, as if ready for a fight, but Ariana didn't move. Before her was a raging fire, lit in the center of a clearing in otherwise dense woods. The tree line was marked off by a ring of thick, well-worn gravestones, each with a name etched into it, though Ariana couldn't make them out in the dim light. The fire pit was circumscribed by dozens of perfectly round, whitish-gray rocks.

No. Not stones, Ariana realized upon second glance. Skulls. Dozens of human skulls.

Standing on one side of the fire was a tall, broad figure dressed in full-on black, his face covered over by a black ski mask, his hands behind his back. On the other side was a smaller, more feminine person, dressed exactly the same. Each of them stood behind a gravestone. The guy's read LEAR. The girl's, MISS TEMPLE.

Ariana's terror drained away as she took all of this in, replaced by an overwhelming rush of excitement. It was one of the secret societies. It had to be. She wasn't going to be arrested. She was not going to be shot. She was, in fact, being tapped.

And so was Kaitlynn.

"Okay, this is freaky. Even for the government," Kaitlynn said.

Ariana shot Kaitlynn a silencing glare and saw that she, Brigit, Tahira, and Allison were all standing in a line next to her.

So Tahira is not *in the society . . . yet,* Ariana thought. *Interesting.*

She looked around at the other gravestones nearby, each inscribed with a name from classic literature—Jay Gatsby, Elizabeth Bennett, Captain Ahab, and on and on. Both Lear and Miss Temple stood behind their stones. Did that mean the other members were standing behind theirs as well, in the trees, just out of sight? The very idea that she was surrounded by lurking secret society members, her every move being watched, made Ariana's heart pound.

"We are the Stone and Grave." The two figures spoke suddenly, in unison. "You have been brought here tonight as a mark of your potential. Now you must prove your worthiness to the brotherhood. Only the courageous of heart and the strong of mind should accept this challenge. Do you accept?"

"I do," Tahira and Brigit said quickly.

Ariana was still too exhilarated to formulate a thought.

"Speak up, neophytes!" one of the figures barked. "Do you accept this challenge?"

"I do!" All five of them answered this time.

"Very well."

Lear walked around his gravestone and took a step forward. He paced before the five girls, looking them up and down. Ariana stared at his eyes, trying to discern whether she had seen them before, but they were entirely unfamiliar. Disappointment welled inside her chest.

She had believed Palmer was the president of the secret society, had assumed that he would be the one running this game.

"Stone and Grave is a hallowed institution," Lear began, the fire crackling behind him, giving him a menacing air. "We are about loyalty, humanity, bravery, selflessness, brotherhood. Our bonds are unbreakable. We rise as one, and as one we fall. Our membership runs deep in the veins of this country, in every university, every industry, every branch of government. As a member of Stone and Grave, your success in this world is guaranteed."

Ariana glanced over at Brigit, whose attention was trained on Lear. Her entire being hummed with hope and pride. This was exactly what she needed. The Stone and Grave was the final piece of the puzzle. Get in and she would achieve everything she wanted. Get in and her past was erased.

"Pledge your allegiance to Stone and Grave, and Stone and Grave will pledge its allegiance to you," Lear said, pausing in the center of the clearing. The fire hissed and popped as it consumed a tree branch. Lear brought his fists together in front of him, forming a circle with his arms. "Stone and Grave will celebrate you in times of prosperity, protect you in times of trouble, provide for you in times of need. All the brotherhood asks for is your unwavering loyalty."

God, this was perfect. Ariana couldn't have conjured up anything better herself. She wondered if the other girls were as giddy as she was, practically unable to stand still.

"Sister?" he said, glancing over his shoulder.

Miss Temple stepped forward. She cleared her throat before she spoke. "Each of you has been deemed a potential by the brotherhood, but our membership is exclusive and finite." She had a high voice. Unusually high. And nasal. As if she was trying to disguise what she really sounded like. "We have only four open spots for female neophytes. Four spots, five of you. Therefore, you each must complete a task in order to prove your worthiness to the brotherhood. "

As she spoke, Lear walked down the line of neophytes, handing each of them a small black envelope. Ariana was breathless with anticipation and already her mind was trying to rank her chances against the other neophytes. Certainly she could prove herself more worthy than Allison and Tahira. And even Brigit, if she was being honest. She was stronger than any of them. Smarter. Quicker. A survivor. Whatever task the secret society had chosen for her, she was going to master it.

But Kaitlynn was a survivor, too. Ariana was certain the girl would be in Stone and Grave by the time this was over. The very thought of this—the thought of being tied to Kaitlynn for life—made Ariana's stomach revolt. She had to swallow back the bile that rose up in her throat.

"You must complete these tasks by the second Sunday of September to be considered for membership, but merely completing them will not guarantee your acceptance," Lear stated. "The brotherhood will be watching you. If you try to take the easy way out, we will know. If your execution lacks creativity, we will know. It's not just about the end result, it's about the means."

The girl stepped forward again. "We will meet again on that

Sunday, and your work will be evaluated. If you have not completed your task by then, you will automatically be blackballed. If you have not completed your task in a way that is satisfactory to the brotherhood, you will also be blackballed." The fire waved behind her, casting her body in shadow. "Stone and Grave does not tap seniors, which means this is your final chance to impress the brotherhood," she said, looking right at Brigit and Tahira. Both of them simply stared back, still as stone.

Ariana blinked. She remembered what Lexa had said that day in the library. That it was Brigit's last chance to get into the society, implying that she had been tapped before and had failed. Had the same happened with Tahira?

"You are not to show these cards to anyone," Lear intoned, stepping back into line with his counterpart. Ariana was certain she heard swishing behind her. Footfalls behind the trees. Snapping branches. The other members *were* out there watching. She was certain of it. And now they were on the move. "You are not to share what you've heard here tonight. You are not to speak of this night to anyone outside your circle of five. Betrayal is a sin that is not taken lightly by the brotherhood. If you turn your back on Stone and Grave, if you malign Stone and Grave, if you allow civilians to learn the secrets of Stone and Grave, you will be dealt with. We take these crimes seriously. *Dead* seriously."

Ariana's throat closed over. She remembered how freaked Lexa had been that day when she'd slipped and told Ariana about the society. What, exactly, did he mean by "dealt with"? Ariana glanced around at

Kaitlynn, Brigit, Tahira, and Allison, all of whom looked as uncertain as Ariana felt.

"Your time to impress the brotherhood starts now," Miss Temple said.

Then she and Lear snuffed out the fire, pitching the clearing into darkness. The movement in the trees intensified for a moment, and then all was silent. Ariana's breath came short and shallow. She couldn't see a thing.

"We suggest you start walking before the black bears get a whiff of you." Lear's voice carried back to them through the night. "Good luck!"

TREK

"Are you sure we're going the right way?" Allison demanded, her German accent thicker than usual, probably due to panic.

"This is a well-worn path," Kaitlynn pointed out for the tenth time. "And this is definitely the direction we came in from."

"Doesn't seem like much of a path to me. It's too narrow," Tahira said with a sniff. Her high heels kept sinking into the soft earth, so she was lagging behind. "And how do you know which direction we came from? We were all blindfolded."

Ariana and Brigit, who were walking side by side in the dark, occasionally grabbing each other's hands when they stumbled or tripped, shot one another an amused look. Tahira was being Tahira. As always.

"If you want to go off on your own, I'm not stopping you," Kaitlynn replied. "Woods, meet Tahira; Tahira, meet the woods. Go ahead."

Tahira crossed her arms over her chest. "You don't have to be such a bitch about it."

Kaitlynn paused and dropped her arms. "I'm sorry, T, okay? It's just I want to get back to campus and get started on my task just like you do. So let's just work together."

Ariana smirked. She knew that Kaitlynn would have loved to tear into Tahira, but *Lillian* couldn't turn Tahira into an enemy, just in case she needed her later.

"Fine," Tahira said finally, walking ahead, her ankles wobbling. "What is your task anyway?"

Allison shoved a pine branch aside. "I don't know if we should be sharing tasks."

"She's right. I think I'll keep mine to myself, thanks," Kaitlynn said.

"What does yours say?" Brigit whispered to Ariana, leaning close.

"It's too dark out here. I can't make it out," Ariana replied.

"Here," Brigit said. "You can use this."

She lifted her wrist and pushed a few rubber bracelets away from her chunky watch. With a click of a button, the face illuminated big and bright. Ariana stopped walking, pulled out her card, and tilted the watch face toward it. There, in silver ink, was her task:

MAKE A SPECTACLE OF YOURSELF

Ariana's heart dove. "What? Are they kidding?"

Brigit snorted a laugh when she read it. "Mine says, 'Embarrass the crown prince of Jordan at the NoBash.'"

"But I thought—" Ariana paused, unsure how many of her theories and how much of her knowledge she should reveal. Then again, Brigit had obviously been tapped before. She had to know even more than Ariana did.

"You thought what?" Brigit asked as they speed walked to catch up with the others.

"I kind of thought Lexa was in Stone and Grave," Ariana whispered. Not to mention Palmer, whom she had assumed was president or leader or grand poobah or whatever they called the number one Stone and Graver. She couldn't believe he would set her up to embarrass herself. "Couldn't she have made sure it was something less . . . horrible?"

Brigit pressed her lips together in a knowing way that made Ariana's skin prickle. "Stone and Grave wants what it wants," she said cryptically, lifting her shoulders.

Ariana sighed. She hated when other people knew more than she did. But in this particular case, it might be better for her not to dig too deep. At least not yet. But why make a spectacle of herself, when all Brigit had to do was embarrass someone else? It seemed completely unfair.

"Hey Ana, can you come up here a sec?" Kaitlynn shouted from her place at the head of the group.

Ariana bit her tongue to keep from cursing the girl out.

"I'll be back," she said to Brigit.

She maneuvered her way past Tahira and Allison, who were also whispering to each other, and joined Kaitlynn at the front of the group. The trees were growing thicker, the underbrush encroaching on the dirt path, and Ariana was starting to seriously doubt that this was, in fact, the way they'd come.

"What do you want?" Ariana asked under her breath. Something tickled her ankle and she told herself it was just a twig or a weed, and not a spider.

"Yeah, listen, I obviously need to be in Stone and Grave so I'm thinking, to make it easier for everyone, you should just drop out of the running," Kaitlynn said quietly, her gaze dead ahead.

Ariana laughed. "Pardon me if I don't dignify that with a response."

"What's so funny?" Tahira asked from a few yards back.

"Nothing!" Kaitlynn sang in reply, upping her speed slightly so that Ariana had to jog in the dark to keep up.

"It's only fair, A," Kaitlynn continued, her tone diplomatic. She lowered her voice so that it was barely audible over the sound of their crunching steps. "You're set. You've got an identity, a trust fund, a future, but me . . . I've got two years to make connections that will take me beyond APH. I'm going to need these guys to help me do that."

"You really think that once you're in and they figure out that Lillian Oswald has no background whatsoever, they're going to *help* you create one?" Ariana asked. She struggled to catch her breath. Between the exercise, the nerve-racking darkness, and this conversation, she was starting to perspire. "They'll probably just boot you back to the Brenda T.," she said through her teeth.

"You heard what they said. If you're a member, they protect you. They shelter you. And they're insanely connected," Kaitlynn replied. "So yes, I do think they'll help me."

Ariana sighed. This should be a platinum night for her. But instead, she was dealing with Kaitlynn's psychosis. Again. She glanced over her shoulder to make sure no one could hear them. The others were so far behind now that she could barely hear them, let alone see them.

"I'm not dropping out," she said flatly.

"Okay then, plan B. Who should we bump off?" Kaitlynn said, pushing a thick branch aside and letting it snap back in Ariana's face. The pain was sharp but fleeting. Ariana spit a few pine needles off her lips as she rushed to catch up.

"Bump off?" Ariana hissed. "Are you serious?"

Kaitlynn gave a look that told Ariana that she was, in fact, very serious.

"I'm not going to *kill* anyone," Ariana replied.

"Okay, then maybe I'll just kill you," Kaitlynn said with a shrug. Ariana's heart caught, and she misstepped, tripping forward and almost falling flat on her face. Annoyingly, she had to grab on to Kaitlynn, the very person who'd just threatened her life, to keep from going down.

"Watch it. There's a bit of a hill here," Kaitlynn said, a laugh in her voice.

Sure enough, the ground was dropping away beneath them, and their steps naturally quickened. If she shoved Kaitlynn as hard as she could right now, no one would see it. But Kaitlynn would have to fall just so in order to break her neck, and if she didn't, she would certainly tell everyone how she'd been pushed.

Why couldn't they just stumble upon a nice, convenient cliff?

"You do realize that if something happens to me, they're going to find you out," Ariana hissed, her heart pounding.

"Maybe," Kaitlynn replied, glancing back as the footsteps behind them—and Tahira's cursing under her breath—grew closer. "But killing you could get me everything I want. Then again, if I *don't* kill you and I *don't* get into Stone and Grave, in two years, I'm out on the street with nothing."

It was amazing to Ariana how cavalierly she spoke about murder. And to the very person whose life she was planning on ending.

"Why does everything come back to murder with you?" Ariana whispered, her feet pounding the ground. Her ankle twisted slightly as she stepped on a rock, but this time she bit her lip and found her own balance, not wanting to rely on Kaitlynn again. "Maybe one of them will screw up their task or not perform it with enough flair. You heard what Miss Temple said. That would mean an automatic blackball."

"Yes, but I can't count on that," Kaitlynn said. "I'd much rather have the guarantee of an open spot. Then as long as I do what I need to do, I'll get in."

"Okay, then why not just sabotage someone? Screw up their chances. You don't have to *kill* everyone."

"Look who's talking," Kaitlynn said with a knowing smile. "But you make a good point. Sabotaging someone would work. So get on that, will you?" she said, slapping Ariana on the shoulder.

"What happened to 'we'?" Ariana said, Not that she savored the thought of working side-by-side with Kaitlynn, but this *was* Kaitlynn's idea.

"Come on, A. I have *so* much to deal with right now," Kaitlynn said, holding a thick branch aside. "Making friends, taking placement exams, getting caught up in class, and now I have some crazy task to complete. Help a friend out."

Her tone was so faux-sweet it made Ariana's teeth hurt.

"I'll see what I can do," Ariana said grudgingly.

"Good. And no pressure. I mean, if the sabotage thing doesn't work out, I can always just get rid of you . . . or maybe one of your little friends. Then I'll be a shoo-in," Kaitlynn said brightly.

"Leave my friends out of this," Ariana said, her fists clenching defensively. "Besides, you don't know if any of them are in Stone and Grave."

"Oh, I'm sure I'll be able to figure it out," Kaitlynn singsonged. "In case you haven't noticed, *Ana*, I'm kind of a genius when it comes to people."

She paused as they came to a clearing at the edge of the woods. Before them, the hill dropped down toward the merrily twinkling lights of the campus below.

"Oh, look," Kaitlynn said, lifting a hand. "I got us home."

"Nice work, Lily," Tahira said happily, emerging from the woods and wrapping her arm through Kaitlynn's. Clearly she had forgotten all about her earlier grumblings. "Let's go grab a midnight snack. I'm all about chocolate at this hour—how about you?"

"Definitely," Kaitlynn replied as the two of them traipsed down the hill. "It's going to be so much fun when we're in Stone and Grave together," Kaitlynn said. "You and I are going to just take over."

Their laughter mingled on the breeze as the gap between them and Ariana widened.

"Wait for me!" Allison shouted, jogging after them.

Brigit finally tripped her way out of the woods and came to stop at Ariana's side. Ariana was frozen in place, stunned by Kaitlynn's total disregard for everything, her own security included. What was she going to do, slit Ariana's throat in the middle of the night? Wouldn't the roommate be the obvious suspect in a crime like that?

But that was the problem. Kaitlynn was insane. There was no telling what she was capable of.

"Everything okay?" Brigit asked.

"Yeah . . . yes," Ariana said, waking herself up from her dark thoughts. "It will be."

Everything was going to be fine, as soon as Ariana arranged some insurance for herself. Something that would make it impossible for Kaitlynn to hurt her without hurting herself.

"Come on." She slung her arm through Brigit's just as Tahira had done with Kaitlynn. "I think we deserve a celebratory dessert from the café."

"But my diet—"

"Forget your diet. We just got tapped. I say we let loose for one night," Ariana said. "Have you seen that triple-chocolate tart they have? I bet it's to die for."

"Oh, I am so very in," Brigit said happily. "Just don't tell Soomie and Maria, okay? They'll torture me about it."

"Don't worry. I'm good at keeping secrets," Ariana said, watching Kaitlynn bound down the hill arm-in-arm with Tahira. *Very* good."

THE WEAKEST LINK

"We are definitely going to be late for French," Soomie said, glancing at her BlackBerry on Wednesday morning.

"Yes, but it's so worth it," Ariana replied. Maria nodded her agreement.

They were kicked back on three of the cushy lounge chairs situated on the patio outside the Wolcott Hall café. The airy, flagstone square was dotted with planters full of brightly colored mums and flourishing Japanese maples, their deep red leaves backlit by the sunshine. There were a few students at the various tables, leafing through textbooks and indulging in croissants and scones. Behind them, down the hill from the house, the wide Potomac River burbled along peacefully. It was all so perfect it seemed impossible that it could be real.

And horrible to think that it could all be taken away. Ariana had been up all night, thinking about this whole sabotage idea, and she'd come up with one tiny problem: Presumably, the members of Stone and Grave were watching the potential members at all times. Which meant that if she sabotaged someone, they would see it. Wouldn't they sort of frown on the kind of behavior? If they were all about the brotherhood and mutual support, wouldn't sabotaging someone disqualify her?

"Where is that girl already?" Maria asked. "I need my caffeine."

"No, really?" Soomie joked, flicking her dark hair over her shoulder.

"What else is new?" Ariana added.

Having skipped breakfast that morning in favor of sleeping in, they had decided to grab coffee and pastries at the café before class. Or, rather, have others grab coffee and pastries *for* them. Lexa had been up at the crack of dawn for her daily run, and Brigit was on a phone call with the king and queen.

"Here you go, Ana. One iced skim latte with a dash of cinnamon."

Ariana looked up at Quinn, the sophomore who was on twenty-four-hour coffee duty for Lexa, Maria, Soomie, Brigit, and now Ariana. Lexa really had Atherton-Pryce Hall wired. Before the school year had even started she had locked down a whole troop of sophomores who were at the beck and call of her and her friends. Quinn and her counterparts, Melanie and Jessica, had all been on Team Gold and therefore all had access to Privilege House. Having them around was going to make everything that much easier. Noelle Lange would have been so impressed.

"Thanks, Quinn," Ariana said, taking the ice-cold plastic cup and sipping at the straw. She smiled happily, glad of one perk she didn't have to share with Kaitlynn. At least not yet.

"An espresso for Maria," Quinn continued, handing over the drink. Maria grabbed it like she was lost in the desert and it was the last cup of water on earth. "And a chai tea and an almond scone for Soomie."

"Thanks," the other girls said, giving their lackey brief smiles.

"Anything else before I go to Italian?" Quinn asked, quickly checking her Gucci watch. Her straight red hair was back in a tortoiseshell headband and she wore her uniform all tucked and pristine. Ariana appreciated the sophomore's attention to detail. When she got into Stone and Grave she was going to keep an eye on Quinn for potential membership.

"We're fine," Soomie said, taking a sip of her tea. "Don't be late on our account."

"Okay. Have a good day!" Quinn said before grabbing her overstuffed backpack and walking off.

Ariana leaned back in the chair and tried to relax—tried to think of something to chat about with her friends—but all that kept coming to mind was Kaitlynn and her death threats. After partaking in the Stone and Grave ceremony the night before, Ariana was more determined than ever to get in. But that would require three things—first, not getting murdered by Kaitlynn; second, not letting Kaitlynn murder any of her friends; and third, being one of the four who got in, rather than the one poor soul who did not.

A pair of songbirds twittered in one of the nearby trees, and Ariana wondered sadly at the fact that she had to be thinking about murder at all on a gorgeous day such as this.

It was too bad she couldn't ask for Soomie and Maria's advice. Find out if she was right about sabotage being a no-no to the Stone and Gravers. She had a feeling they were both in Stone and Grave already, and might have some useful advice, but she couldn't even tell them about the tapping ceremony the night before without risking Stone and Grave's wrath, let alone revealing the truth about herself and Kaitlynn.

Unless . . . . maybe she could ask them without really asking them. They would obviously know what she was talking about, but would probably answer without acknowledging it. At least, that was what Ariana would do for them if she was in and they were out.

"Ana, what is your problem?" Maria said suddenly. "You've sighed ten times in the last five minutes."

"Have I? Sorry," Ariana replied. "Just having deep thoughts."

"Anything we can help with?" Soomie asked.

"I wish," Ariana replied.

She took a deep breath of the early-autumn air. Should she give it a try, or would Stone and Grave consider even thinly veiled questions to be a crime?

"Try us," Maria said finally.

Ariana shifted in her seat. She decided to trust her friends. Trust that they wouldn't report her to Stone and Grave. If there was ever a time to rely on their friendship, it was now.

"It's just . . . there's something I want . . . and there are a bunch of people standing in the way of me getting it," Ariana said. "And I'm not sure how to deal with it."

There. Technically, she hadn't said a word about Stone and Grave, so technically she had broken no rules. Soomie and Maria exchanged a glance.

"That's easy," Maria said, sliding her sunglasses atop her head.

"Take out the weakest link," Soomie said.

Ariana felt a sizzle of possibility skitter through her heart. She'd known she could count on them. And here they were, practically suggesting sabotage outright. So maybe it wasn't going to get her disqualified.

"The weakest link," she repeated.

Just then the glass doors behind them opened and out traipsed Tahira and Allison. They gabbed and laughed obnoxiously all the way across the patio to a table shaded by a red umbrella. Once seated, they attacked their apple-cinnamon muffins like a pair of rabid dogs let loose in a chicken coop. So unsavory.

Of course, Ariana could have turned it around on Kaitlynn and simply sabotaged *her*. Taking Kaitlynn out of the running would not only mean getting into Stone and Grave, but it would also mean Kaitlynn would not be there to annoy her all the time. But there was a problem with that plan. If she sabotaged Kaitlynn, then Kaitlynn might turn her in to the authorities—or worse, kill her.

The only option was to take someone else out. Then both she and Kaitlynn would get what they wanted. Mostly. Ariana would still have to deal with being tied to Kaitlynn for life, but at least she'd be in. And alive.

"The weakest link. The person who doesn't have the guts or the brains to fight back," Soomie added, scrolling through her e-mails on her BlackBerry.

Okay. Now they were definitely condoning sabotage. There was no question about it. Ariana stared at Tahira and Allison. She had already crossed Tahira, and the girl not only had a temper, but as daughter of the leader of Dubai, she had connections like no one else on campus—except maybe Brigit. She was definitely not the weakest link. But Allison . . . what did Allison really have going for her? She was pretty, sure. Athletic, definitely. Came from money—but who around here didn't?

Target acquired.

And Ariana knew just what to do. When she had wanted to clear a space in Billings House for Reed Brennan so that she could keep an eye on her 24/7, she had engineered a cheating scandal that had gotten Leanne Shore booted off campus. It had been so easy, Ariana could have done it blindfolded with one hand tied behind her back. So why not do that again? Allison didn't even have to get thrown out of school. She just needed to do something serious enough that Stone and Grave would take notice. Something they would consider unacceptable. Cheating still worked. It was a classic. The society wouldn't want to accept anyone who had been caught cheating and been publicly embarrassed.

Suddenly Ariana felt more confident, relaxed, and happy than she had all night. Obviously Maria and Soomie knew what she was talking about, and obviously they wanted to help her get in to Stone and Grave. They had truly accepted her.

"Thanks, you guys. I really appreciate it," Ariana said meaning-fully.

"Anytime," Soomie said, brushing Ariana's arm with her fingers.

"But really, Ana, you don't need our advice," Maria said, draining her cup before she stood. "You clearly have a talent for getting what you want. Getting into APH *and* Privilege House is no easy feat."

Ariana's heart skipped a beat. There was something in Maria's tone she didn't like. Something knowing.

"Thanks," Ariana said, trying to read Maria's face as she rose from her chair.

"My father always says that you only need three things to succeed in life," Soomie intoned, slinging her black messenger bag over her shoulder. "One, ambition; two, intelligence; and three, a really good lawyer."

Ariana and Maria laughed as they made their way through the doors, headed for the front exit and the hill beyond. It was just para-noia, she was sure. How could Maria possibly know anything about Ariana's real past? As far as anyone here knew, she was Briana Leigh Covington. No one had any reason to question that.

Right?

DEADLINE

As soon as the end-of-class tone came through the loudspeaker in history that afternoon, Ariana was up and out of her seat, her jaw clenched in annoyance. She had been looking forward to the class, history being one of her favorite subjects, but she hadn't been able to enjoy one second of it. During the entire fifty-five-minute class she had absorbed exactly zero knowledge. The moment Kaitlynn had walked through the door and handed her placement slip to Ms. Ferren, Ariana's shoulder muscles had coiled and her brain had flipped into thought-racing mode.

There had been no concentrating, no relaxing, no learning. It was all about Kaitlynn's breath on her neck. Her citrusy perfume choking the air. Her hand brushing Ariana's hair every time she raised her hand to answer a question. By the time the class was over Ariana was in serious need of a massage, a soothing yoga class, and an hour in a warm, lavender-scented bath. Then, perhaps, she would be able to breathe.

"Hey Ana!" Kaitlynn called out in the hallway. "Wait up!"

Ariana kept walking, nearly tripping over some hapless freshman who had dropped his books in the middle of the hall. She turned up the speed as she headed for the stairwell. Not that it mattered. Kaitlynn was at her side in no time.

"Aren't you psyched we're in the same class? I took the history test on Monday morning and they're letting me join my classes as my results come in so I don't miss too much," she babbled.

"Why you think I care about any of this is beyond me," Ariana said, her eyes fierce as she glared over her shoulder.

She turned sideways to make more room for the overweight professor coming toward her and scurried down the stairs. Kaitlynn paused for a moment at the top but soon recovered and jogged to catch up.

"Where are you rushing off to?"

"The appropriate question is, 'What am I rushing away *from*?'" Ariana said through her teeth. Her hand gripped the oak railing on the stairs, steadying her steps as her body quaked with anger. Was it too much to ask that Kaitlynn at least not be placed in her classes? Between being her roommate and competing with her for a spot in Stone and Grave, she had to deal with the bitch enough already.

"Very funny," Kaitlynn said drily.

Maybe I should just trip her. Just put out my foot and trip her. With any luck she'll crack her skull on the marble and this will all be over. An accident. It would look like a total freak accident. Maybe I could even give her a push.

Her foot flinched outward as Kaitlynn caught up with her, but she only succeeded in kicking the ankle of a tall, gawky boy in glasses.

"Ow. Watch it."

"Sorry," Ariana said, blushing. She hit the landing and kept moving, feeling hot an annoyed and stupid. Tripped on the stairs. Right. As if that would work. Stupid, Ariana. Stupid, stupid, stupid. She gripped her forearm and squeezed.

"So, have you figured out a sabotage plan yet?" Kaitlynn whispered as Ariana shoved through the heavy doors of the class building.

"I'm working on it," Ariana said, stepping quickly down the stone steps and onto the main green at the center of campus.

"Really? Because I thought I saw you reposing on the patio with your little friends this morning," Kaitlynn replied, keeping a friendly smile on her face for the rest of the world to see. "Didn't look like you were working too hard to me."

"Look, I have a plan. I just have to figure out how I'm going to execute it," Ariana said, pausing under a huge cherry tree. "Give me some time."

Kaitlynn took a deep breath and blew it out through her nose impatiently. "If I give you time it might never get done," she said, holding her notebook to her chest. "So how about a deadline? You've always worked well under deadlines."

Ariana tensed, reminded of how much Kaitlynn knew about her past. She'd known that the Fourth of July was the only day her escape from the Brenda T. could have happened, and how Ariana had made sure everything was in place before then. She knew that Ariana had found a way to raise a million dollars to pay Kaitlynn off in just a week. The girl knew way too much. Arian's grip on her forearm tightened. Then a pair of girls she recognized from Wolcott walked by and she forced a smile.

"You have ten days. Until the night of the NoBash. If you don't eliminate someone by then, *I* will," she said, her eyes menacing. She glanced around the circle and spotted Maria, Soomie, Lexa, Landon, and Adam chatting near the fountain. "All we need is one more open spot. I wonder which one of your little buddies it'll be. Let's see. Well, obviously Lexa is in. The queen bee is *always* in. And she probably wouldn't room with Maria unless she was in as well. Soomie would *have* to be in, since she's the number one brain around here. She seems pretty scrappy, though. She'd probably put up a fight."

Ariana pressed her lips together. All around her students were chatting and lounging and going over notes. Having normal lives. Just like Ariana was supposed to be doing. But instead, she was faced with this. With this constant pressure and the never-ending threats. This was not the way it was supposed to be.

"Or will it be you?" Kaitlynn added, gazing into Ariana's eyes hungrily, as if she was simply salivating for the chance to kill again. Ariana shuddered. Kaitlynn was even more insane than she'd ever imagined. Was it possible that she *wanted* Ariana to fail? Wanted an excuse to commit a pointless murder? Didn't she know that murder was no game? That it was only to be used as a last resort?

God, she's crazy, Ariana thought. *She deserves to be in the Brenda T. Why, why, why did I get her out?*

"Fine," Ariana said through her teeth. "By the night of the NoBash, there will only be four of us in contention. In the meantime, back off my friends," she said firmly.

Kaitlynn's eyebrows rose in surprise—or was it respect?—at the demand. "Right. Whatever you say."

"Hey Ana!" Lexa called out from the other side of the circle. "My dad's taking us out for lunch in Georgetown. You coming?"

Ariana smiled as Kaitlynn's face fell.

"Absolutely!" Ariana replied.

"Good! Let's go!" Lexa said, tilting her head. "He's dying to meet the infamous Briana Leigh Covington."

"Okay!" Ariana replied. She looked at Kaitlynn, feeling suddenly calm, and very superior. "Guess you're not invited. Sorry, *Lily.*"

Ariana brushed by Kaitlynn, pulling her thick auburn hair over her shoulder and away from her neck, attempting to cool her body temperature.

"Oh, Ana?"

Ariana paused. She took a deep breath and turned around to face her nemesis.

"Speaking of invitations, don't forget I'll also be needing an invite to that party," Kaitlynn said. "The sooner the better. There are plans to be made."

Ariana smiled sweetly. She loved a perfect opening. "No worries, Lily. If you're too pathetic to make your own friends, I'll do what I can to help you."

Kaitlynn frowned and Ariana quickly walked off to join Lexa and the rest of her crew. She made a big show of throwing her arm around Lexa's shoulders as they headed for the pickup/drop-off area on the far side of the dorms, knowing Kaitlynn was watching. There. Let her stew over that for a while.

At least she'd found a way to get rid of that smirk—for the moment.

RIGID

It was way past time to assume control of the situation.

As Ariana stalked across the circle and up the hill toward Wolcott Hall, her blood boiled hotter with each step. She had just sat through what should have been a lovely lunch with Lexa's father, Senator Greene, and her friends, but she hadn't been able to enjoy it because she couldn't stop thinking about her encounter with Kaitlynn. The girl had ruined a perfectly good social outing and she hadn't even *been* there. Ariana knew that if she was ever going to get her emotions in check, she had to act. Had to put some plan in motion that would fix at least one, if not all, of her current troubles. First things first: Remove Allison from the running for Stone and Grave. Save her friends' lives and her own. After she got that plot started, she could concentrate on what would hopefully be the easier task, securing an invite to the NoBash for Kaitlynn.

Then she could deal with getting Lexa and Conrad together. And her own task for Stone and Grave—making a spectacle of herself. That was going to be interesting. How in the world was she supposed to do that? Wear her underwear on the outside of her uniform for a day? Don last season's shoes? Shave her head? Not one of these ideas appealed. What were they looking for? How devastating a humiliation were they expecting?

Ariana had come to the top of the hill and was walking so fast she found herself panting unattractively.

Breathe. Focus.

The Allison Plan. That was why she was here. Because all good plotters needed willing lackeys. Brigit hadn't been at lunch because she had a gown fitting for the NoBash. Ariana hoped to find her friend in her room. She shoved through the doors of Wolcott and almost slammed into Tahira and Allison.

"Watch it!" Tahira snapped. "You almost took my head off!"

If only, Ariana thought, sliding past them without a word, her teeth clenched.

"God. Sweat much?" Allison commented, looking Ariana up and down with disgust. She and Tahira cracked up laughing and continued through the door. Ariana felt like she was going to spontaneously combust.

Yes, Allison had to go. As soon as humanly possible.

Breathing in deeply through her nose and out through her mouth, Ariana took the elevator to the top floor. By the time she got there she felt much calmer. She knocked on the closed door of Soomie and Brigit's room. There was a scuffle and some urgent whispering.

"Who is it?" Brigit called.

"It's Ana."

"Are you alone?"

Ariana glanced behind her at the empty hallway.

"Yes. Is something wrong?"

"No. Come in. Quickly."

Ariana slipped inside the room. Brigit was stepping onto a seamstresses' block wearing a royal purple gown of pure, shimmering silk. It had cap sleeves and a square neckline that framed her neck and face perfectly. Very flattering. Crouching at Brigit's feet, pinning the hem, was a diminutive woman with graying brown hair pulled back in a bun.

"Hey, Ana. Sorry about that," Brigit said, all flushed. "I just can't let Tahira or Allison see my gown. How was lunch?"

"It was great, but we missed you," Ariana replied, placing her bag on Soomie's bed. "What a beautiful dress."

"I know, isn't it?" Brigit's face was giddy with pleasure. "Leah's a genius. Oh! How rude of me. Ana, this is Leah. She just got in from Oslo this morning."

Ariana tried not to let her envy reflect in her eyes. Personal seamstress flown in from Norway? What a life.

"A pleasure to meet a friend of the princess." Leah rose to her feet and shook Ariana's hand—a tight, bony grip—and bowed her head slightly.

"The pleasure's mine," Ariana replied. "You do amazing work."

"Thank you, miss."

Leah got right back to work, dropping to her knees and edging her way around Brigit's skirt.

"Do you have a gown yet?" Brigit asked excitedly.

"No, actually," Ariana replied, realizing she was going to have to use her emergency credit card to secure a proper outfit for the NoBash. That was going to be fun to explain to Grandma Covington.

"Well, you'd better get on that soon," Brigit warned. Then her eyes lit up. "I know! Why don't we go shopping together? This Saturday? We'll get everyone together. It'll be so much fun!"

Ariana grinned. The idea of a shopping excursion with friends almost negated the irritating thought of putting on Briana Leigh's particular begging whine and explaining the charge to her crotchety grandmother.

"Okay. Sounds like a plan," she said.

"Good. So . . . what's up?" Brigit asked. "You look all flushed." Her blue eyes brightened again and she clasped her hands in front of her. "Is it a boy? Did you meet someone? Did I tell you I asked Adam to the NoBash? He said yes!"

Ariana laughed. "That's great, Brigit. I knew he would. But no. No boys for me." *Yet,* she added silently. "Actually, I was just wondering . . . how do you feel about pranks?"

Brigit's grin widened. "I love them. As long as they're not being played on me."

"Of course. No one likes those," Ariana said with a smile.

She strolled over to Brigit's side of the room where there were a dozen framed photos hung around her bed. Some of the pictures featured Brigit dressed up in designer gowns, sporting to-die-for jewels and tiaras, posing with young dignitaries and celebrities from around the world. But then there was a pic of Brigit and her parents in hiking gear, posing on a ledge at the side of a mountain. Another of her and her dad in a canoe somewhere, smiling at the photographer, looking for all the world like a perfectly normal father and daughter, rather than a king and his princess daughter.

"Who are we pranking?" Brigit asked.

"Allison," Ariana replied.

"Ooooh! Then I am totally in," Brigit replied. "Is this for the . . . you-know-what?" she asked in a leading voice, glancing down at Leah, who was simply going about her work.

"No," Ariana semi-lied. It wasn't as if Stone and Grave had asked her to prank Allison, but the prank *was* Stone and Grave–related. "She just needs a little payback for being such a bitch when we were living together."

Brigit giggled. "I like it. What's the plan? What do you need me to do?"

Ariana smiled. She knew she'd chosen the right accomplice. Brigit was definitely the kind of girl who lived life to the fullest and knew how to have fun. On the floor, Leah *tsk*ed under her breath.

"Oh, please, Leah. Like you didn't tear it up a little when you were in school," Brigit said. "I'm sure it'll be totally harmless, right, Ana?"

Ariana swallowed hard. "Of course."

"At least save the planning of this thing until I am out of the room," Leah requested, looking up at the princess. "The less I know, the less I will be able to tell if the king starts to ask questions."

Brigit laughed lightly. "Fine. We'll wait."

"Good." Leah placed her last pin. "There. All finished."

Brigit stepped down to the floor and looked at the hem, which was lying flat on the hardwood at her feet. "It's still too long," she pointed out.

"I know. I've done this for a reason," Leah said, shoving an extra pin into the cushion she had strapped to her wrist.

Brigit's posture collapsed. "Oh, no, Leah. Don't tell me you're going to get on me about this *again!*"

"About what?" Ariana asked.

"The princess does not know how to walk in high heels," Leah told Ariana. "I keep trying to tell her that a woman in her position needs to know how to walk in heels, but does she listen to me, a woman who has been dressing royals for over twenty years? No."

"What's the big deal?" Brigit asked. "God made me this height. Why can I not attend parties at the height God made me?"

"Hasn't attended church since she's been in the States, but now she wants to invoke the Lord." Leah rolled her eyes as she stood.

"How do you know that?" Brigit asked, color rising in her cheeks.

"You may think you're far from the prying eyes of your people, your majesty, but the papers back home still print every little thing they can find out about you," Leah said wryly. "Will you talk some sense into the girl?" she asked Ariana, glancing at the heeled boots Ariana was wearing. "Maybe you can give her some pointers. Excuse me for a moment, Princess."

"Of course," Brigit said.

Leah slipped into the bathroom and closed the door behind her. Brigit rolled her eyes.

"She is right, though," Ariana said, looking at Brigit's hem. "Heels say you're a sophisticated woman. If you keep going to parties in flats, it's kind of . . . childish."

"I know, I know," Brigit said, sitting down on the edge of her bed. "But if I start going to parties in heels, I'll be falling all over the place, spilling drinks and dumping cocktail sauce on people. I kind of think that's worse."

"Fair enough," Ariana said, sitting next to her. "So . . . wanna hear the plan?"

"Definitely!" Brigit said, clasping her hands. "I've gotta say, though, I'm kind of surprised at you, Ana Covington," she added, giving Ariana's leg a quick nudge.

"Why? What do you mean?" Ariana asked.

"I don't know . . . I just never would have thought you were the prank type," Brigit said. "Kind of like what Lexa was saying in the bathroom the other day. You're kind of . . ."

She paused and made an apologetic face, as if she didn't want to say what she was actually thinking. All the tiny hairs on Ariana's arms stood on end.

"Kind of what?" she asked, trying not to sound annoyed.

"Um . . . rigid?" Brigit said.

A sour taste filled Ariana's mouth. She felt her fingers start to curl into fists and forced them open again. Rigid? *Rigid?* No. She was not rigid. Just . . . controlled. She had to be controlled. Had to keep herself in check at all times. Had to be careful and calculated. These people had no idea what might happen if she *didn't* maintain that control. Ariana herself had no idea what might happen—a thought that scared her to the very core every time she let it enter. Which was why she had to keep it at bay. Keep every strong emotion—fear, anger, love, lust—under control.

Otherwise, she knew from experience, things could go very, very wrong.

"But not in a bad way," Brigit added quickly. "But I was thinking that maybe that's why Stone and Grave gave you that task." She whispered the words *Stone and Grave*. "You know, so you can prove you can loosen up. That you don't have to take yourself so seriously."

Ariana took a deep, soothing breath. Maybe Brigit was right. And maybe Lexa was the one who had set her task, having already noticed that Briana Leigh wasn't as *Briana Leigh* as she used to be.

"I know how to have fun," Ariana protested. She wished, suddenly, that Brigit and the others could have seen her in her Billings days. Ariana had always been the one to secure the champagne, forge the passes off campus, figure out how to get pastry deliveries in the middle of the night for Fat Phoebe parties. She'd been a total party animal. As long as it was nothing *too* wild. "I threw that party in my room last week, remember?"

"Yes! That was *so* cool," Brigit said, coloring. "Forget I said anything. Obviously I'm wrong. Rigid people do not pull pranks just for fun."

"Exactly," Ariana said, still bristling. She uncurled her fingers and tried to relax. Tried to appear less rigid.

"So. Tell me the plan," Brigit said, getting comfy on her pillows and hopelessly wrinkling her dress. Although, Ariana supposed, Leah would probably just steam the creases out later. "Oh! But before I forget, are you free tonight?"

Ariana blinked. "Aside from studying, sure."

"Good. Meet me and the girls down at the dance studio around eight," she said. "I've got something special planned for Lexa."

"Really? What?" Ariana asked.

"Oh, you'll see," Brigit replied. "I like my events to be a surprise."

Ariana was dying for details but didn't want Brigit to think she was a nosy pain on top of being rigid.

"All right. I'm there," Ariana replied. "Now, on to *my* plan. . . ."

Brigit was all ears and breathless anticipation, and for the first time in a long time Ariana found herself relaxing. Found herself in the middle of a good old-fashioned, lighthearted, mischievous bonding moment.

She was glad Brigit had warned her that she was coming off as tightly wound. Now that she knew it was an issue, she could work on it. She could make sure that her public humiliation proved to the members of Stone and Grave that she was anything *but* rigid. Brigit was a good, honest friend. And it was good to have real friends again.

VERY SOON

After she left Brigit, Ariana headed for the café and a celebratory mocha latte, feeling more herself than she had in days. She'd started the ball rolling. Certainly once the Allison Plan came together, everything else would fall into place as well.

She was just heading past the door to the darkened theater when it flew open right in front of her, two inches from slamming into her skull. An arm reached out, grabbed her by the wrist, and yanked her inside. Ariana was about to scream, until she realized that her assailant was none other than Palmer Liriano.

"Hey," he said quietly, backing her into the wall.

"Hey."

She looked into his warm brown eyes and smiled. He kissed her. A soft, sweet kiss. And this time, she just let it happen, because she knew Lexa was not around. And besides, it felt so very, *very* good.

"Hey," he said again, pulling his face back and smiling.

"You said that already," she replied flirtatiously.

"Sorry. Sometimes when I'm around you I get kind of stupid," Palmer replied.

"Stupid's good," Ariana whispered.

Then she pulled him to her again and kissed him and kissed him and kissed him. His fingers briefly clutched the pleats of her skirt, then slipped beneath the hem, tickling her thigh. Ariana backed toward the wall and Palmer came with, pressing himself up against her so that it felt as every inch of their bodies were touching.

Then he pulled back and cupped her face with his hands. Her lips buzzed as she gazed up at him.

"I told you not to keep me waiting too long," he said. "Now I've had to resort to kidnapping you."

"I know," Ariana said, placing her palms against his chest. He was wearing tan cargo shorts and a gray Yale T-shirt, the letters worn from many washes and a couple of small holes near the hem. Did this mean that Yale was his first choice? And if so, how could she make him switch to Princeton?

It's not about that right now, Ariana.

"I just want to make sure Lexa's over you before we make this thing, you know, public," Ariana said.

"And? How's that going for you?" Palmer asked.

"Brigit's got something planned for tonight, and tomorrow at lunch, I'll be introducing a new man into her life," Ariana said with a smile.

Palmer took a step back. "A new man? Really. Who?"

Ariana's heart panged. He was jealous. Jealous over Lexa. She took a deep breath and told herself it was only natural. He'd been with Lexa for a long time. But then, if he really wanted to be with *her*—Ariana—then why should he care?

"Don't you worry your pretty little head about it," Ariana said, reaching out and tousling his hair because she knew it would probably irk him. But he'd just irked her, so he deserved it. "Now I've got to leave before someone else sneaks in here to hook up and finds us together."

She turned to go.

"Wait."

Ariana smiled to herself. Her heart warmed as he slipped his strong arms around her from behind. At least he did her the courtesy of showing her he wasn't yet ready for her to leave.

"Just tell me it'll be soon," he whispered in her ear. "I don't know how much longer I can keep this up. I think about you all the time and all I want is to be with you. To eat lunch with you, share a study carrel in the library with you, do . . . other things with you . . . ," he added suggestively.

Ariana closed her eyes and let his perfect words rush over her. "Really?" she said, turning around to face him. She lifted his hand so it was palm to palm with hers, then laced their fingers together. "That's all you think about?"

"Don't you?" he asked, looking almost hurt. "I just want to be able to walk across campus with you holding your hand. I want to tell everyone you're my girl." He leaned back and raised his eyebrows. "You *are* my girl, aren't you?"

Ariana felt as if her shoes had just left the floor, like she was actually floating. "Yeah," she said with a smile. "Yeah, I'm your girl."

He squeezed her hand, then lifted the other and held it the same way. "Then tell me it'll be soon."

Ariana smiled. "Soon," she promised, her heart feeling warm and fuzzy and free. "Very soon."

TENSION

"Where're you going?" Kaitlynn asked Ariana as she opened the door of their room that night at exactly 8 p.m. She had estimated that it would take seven minutes for her to get from her room to the dance studio, and she wanted to be fashionably late, but also didn't want to miss out on a single moment of the action. Which meant she had to leave now.

"Nowhere you need to know about," Ariana said, starting through the door.

Kaitlynn shoved herself up off her bed. "You're doing something with *them*, aren't you?" she said, reaching for her jacket. "I'm coming."

Ariana took a deep breath and steeled herself. "No, you're not."

"Why not?" Kaitlynn said in a challenging tone.

Ariana felt as if she were dealing with a child. A small, petulant child. But that was the problem with the insane. It was always "me, me, me" with them. Ariana made a note to remember this when dealing with Kaitlynn from now on. It was just too bad she couldn't put the girl a on permanent time-out.

"Because this is invitation only, and you were not invited," Ariana explained slowly.

"So get me an invitation," Kaitlynn replied.

"I will. I'm getting you an invitation to the NoBash. But in order to do that, it's imperative that you don't start coming off as a needy loser," Ariana said with a sickly sweet smile. "So tonight, I suggest you stay in. See ya!"

She slammed the door of their room, leaving Kaitlynn fuming behind her. As she traipsed out the back door of Wolcott Hall, her head was held high and a triumphant smile played about her lips. Kaitlynn, for once, had not gotten her way.

Ariana arrived at the door of the school's dance studio at exactly 8:08, having been delayed by Kaitlynn for that one minute. The studio was directly across the hallway from the choral room, where the school's select choir was busy running scales, rehearsing for their first concert of the year. Further down the well-lit, marble-floored hallway Ariana could hear a string quartet playing Vivaldi and a guitar plucking away at some antiwar tune from the 1960s. A lone soprano sang a haunting aria that wafted above the other music, asserting itself in the melee.

Ariana took a deep breath. It was such beautiful noise. Such a far cry from the screaming and ranting of the Brenda T. She could listen to it all night long and simply revel in the fact that she was here.

But she had other business to attend to.

Slowly, Ariana opened the door of the dance studio, unsure of what she was going to find. A huge, raucous party? A sophisticated dessert-and-wine gathering? Some kind of *Bachelorette*-style event designed to find Lexa a new beau? (She hoped not, considering she had already chosen one for her.) As soon as she stepped inside, her senses were filled with the scent of eucalyptus and the air rushed in on her like a humid embrace. The pinging sound of soothing spa music tickled her earlobes. An African-American woman in an ocher-colored tunic stepped forward and smiled in a welcoming way.

"You must be Miss Covington. I'm Satia, your masseuse for the evening."

"That, I was not expecting," Ariana said with a pleased laugh.

All the floor-to-ceiling mirrors had been swathed with dark velvet curtains. Ten tall plank fountains stood along the walls, serenely gurgling water into their rock-filled basins. There were five massage tables set up in the center of the room and a few manicure and pedicure stations positioned in the corners. Hovering around the studio were a dozen women dressed just like Satia, smiling placidly, ready to serve. Maria was talking urgently with one of the women near the back wall, while Soomie and Brigit stepped out from behind a Chinese room divider, cinching themselves into comfy-looking moss green robes.

"There you are! What do you think?" Brigit asked, stepping up to Ariana. "Do you think Lexa will like it?"

Just then, the door opened and Lexa walked in, tucking her cell phone into her Birkin bag. Her jaw dropped as she looked around, her eyes wide.

"I think Lexa will *love* it," Lexa said, pulling Brigit in for a hug. "Look at this!" she said, releasing her friend as she took it all in. "This is amazing, Brigit. But what's the occasion?"

"You," Maria said, gliding over to join them. "This is step one in the plan to get your well-toned ass over Palmer Liriano."

"It was all Brigit's idea," Soomie said, giving credit where credit was due. She laid her hand on Brigit's back and Ariana realized it was the first time she'd seen the girl without her BlackBerry surgically attached to her palm.

"Just step one?" Lexa asked, idly picking up a bottle of red nail polish from a nearby counter. "What's step two? A trip to Paris?"

"Not quite," Ariana said, glancing conspiratorially at Maria. "But I think you'll like it."

Ariana had filled Maria in on the Conrad plan between classes and Maria had pounced on the idea. She had said that Connie was one of her favorite people at APH and that she couldn't believe she hadn't thought of him as a match for Lexa before. All of which had left Ariana feeling insightful, triumphant, and hopeful. If Connie turned out to be Lexa's perfect match, then she and Palmer would be free to be together in no time.

"Miss Greene?" the only male masseuse in the room—a tall, gorgeous blond with tan skin and a soap star's smile—gave Lexa a slight bow. "My name is Dirk. If you'd like to get changed, we can get started."

Lexa grinned at Brigit and replaced the nail polish on the counter. "Remind me to buy you something pretty." She took a deep breath and smiled at Dirk. "I'm holding a *lot* of tension in my lower back," she said. "I hope you're ready for a workout."

"Your wish is my command," he said, lifting an arm to guide her toward the room divider and the robes hanging behind. "Shall we?"

"Oh, we shall."

Ariana and her friends dissolved into a giggling fit as Lexa and Dirk walked off together.

"I think this just might work," Ariana said.

"Pardon me while I pat myself on the back," Brigit replied, reaching around to do just that.

"Go ahead and get changed," Soomie said to Ariana. "I bet you could use the relaxation," she added meaningfully.

"Oh, you mean because of what I told you guys this morning?" Ariana said. "I've already taken steps to deal with that situation."

"Good girl," Maria said with a wink.

A warm feeling filled Ariana's heart. Soomie and Maria definitely wanted to see her get into Stone and Grave. They really cared about her. With a swelling surge of pride, Ariana realized what an incredible life she was building for herself here. Real friends, a potential boyfriend, a solid future. Suddenly she felt like patting herself on the back.

"So, Miss Covington," Satia said, accompanying Ariana across the room. "Do you have any particular areas you'd like me to work on? Any muscles holding tension?"

Ariana took a deep breath. "My shoulders and neck, definitely."

Satia tilted her head and looked at Ariana in sympathy. "I find that's the case with a lot of students. All that time spent at the computer."

Ariana smiled. "Yes. That's exactly it."

That and every time I see the murderous psycho who's trying to ruin my life I feel my shoulder muscles twist into pretzels. But you don't need to know about that.

"Omigosh. We should do this every week," Soomie said as her pedicurist massaged the arches of her feet.

A couple of hours without *Kaitlynn every week, being pampered along with my friends?* Ariana thought, slipping into her robe. *I could definitely handle that.*

A GIFT

Ariana awoke on Thursday morning to the dual delights of a bright sunny day and an empty bed opposite her own. Kaitlynn was already up and out, which meant that Ariana could relax as she got ready for classes. She took a deep breath and stretched her arms over her head, recalling the lovely, relaxing evening she'd had the night before. She had felt like a truly integral part of Lexa's group, helping her friends select their nail colors, chatting through their facials and pedicures. Plus her muscles were all perfectly loose this morning. Not a coil or a knot anywhere. All thanks to Brigit. No, thanks to the choice Ariana had made that first morning when she'd arrived at APH. When she'd chosen to be friends with these girls. She had obviously chosen wisely.

With a smile, Ariana allowed herself the luxury of one more minute burrowed under the covers. It was good to be her.

Finally, Ariana opened her eyes and rolled over onto her side. She blinked and lifted her head. There was something sitting on the edge of her night table: a long, pink velvet jewelry box with gold trim, the kind that usually held a necklace or bracelet. Her heart caught. Had Palmer left something for her? Or was this, perhaps, a trinket from Stone and Grave?

Ariana sat up straight and glanced over at Kaitlynn's table. She had no matching box. Which meant either she'd already opened hers, or this was, in fact, something that had been left just for Ariana.

Holding her breath in anticipation, Ariana grabbed up the box and pried it open. Out slipped a long, thick lock of auburn hair. It fluttered to the ground like a leaf, coming to rest on Ariana's bare foot. Instinctively she kicked it off, her nose scrunched in disgust. Then she crouched on the ground for a better look. It was the exact same shade as her own dyed hair.

Her heart dove into her feet and she jumped up, running for the mirror. A strangled cry escaped her throat. There was a big chunk of hair, much more than what had been stashed in the tiny box, chopped away from the right side of her face. Ariana whirled around, her blood hot with anger now, and grabbed the box again. She turned it over, looking for a clue. Nothing. Then she pried the removable bottom out and a folded piece of paper hit the floor. Ariana stooped and unfolded it. It was a small calendar with the word *NoBash* written in red letters over the square for next Saturday, September 14. Yesterday's date was crossed out in red. On the bottom there were three words scrawled in red ink.

NINE DAYS LEFT! ☺

Kaitlynn. Kaitlynn had done this to her while she slept. Ariana hadn't felt a thing. If Kaitlynn could do this to her while she was in her most vulnerable state . . . what else could she do? Ariana stood up, her body quaking, and hurled the box at the wall with a guttural screech, releasing all the anger and fear that had pent up within her chest in the last ten seconds. She imagined herself cramming the box down Kaitlynn's throat, then balling up the calendar and shoving that down there as well. Kaitlynn could not do this to her. She would not let her.

Out in the hallway, a door slammed, and Ariana suddenly realized how much noise she had just made. She looked around her empty room wildly, wondering how many of her floormates had heard. Control. Control was all-important. And she had just lost it.

Just breathe, Ariana.

In, one . . . two . . . three . . .

Out, one . . . two . . . three . . .

In, one . . . two . . . three . . .

Out, one . . . two . . . three . . .

Her heart rate was just returning to normal when a scream split the quiet. Ariana ran out into the hallway and down to Soomie and Brigit's room, where she flung open the door. Soomie was sitting straight up in bed, holding a box just like Ariana's in one hand and a small lock of black hair in the other. Brigit hovered over her, looking horrified.

"Omigod!" Soomie cried, looking up at Ariana. "Do I look as bad as you?"

She got up and ran for the mirror, but it took a minute for her to find the spot where her hair had been chopped. Kaitlynn had taken an inconspicuous lock on the underside of Soomie's hair. A spot that could easily be hidden.

"Who did this?" Soomie cried, her hand shaking.

"Did you get one, too?" Ariana asked Brigit.

Brigit looked around, confused. "No."

"What the hell is this?" Allison shouted.

Ariana exchanged a look with her friends, then rushed down the hall. Allison stood in the center of her room with another box, a blond curl pinched between her finger and thumb. Tahira was nowhere to be found.

"What is going on out here?" Lexa asked, emerging from her room in her robe, freshly showered.

"Someone's gone around chopping off people's hair in the middle of the night," Soomie replied, whirling around.

"What?" Lexa went ashen.

"Allison, Soomie, and Ana all found locks of their hair in boxes by their beds," Brigit explained.

Lexa whirled around and ran back to her room. She emerged a moment later, looking slightly relieved but still freaked. "Maria's gone, but I don't see anything," she said, approaching. She looked over the velvet box in Soomie's hand. "They didn't leave a note or anything?"

Ariana's heart lurched as she thought of the calendar that had been stashed with her lock of hair. She hoped Lexa didn't go looking for her box.

"No. Nothing," Ariana said.

"Who could have done this? And why you three?" Brigit asked.

Lexa narrowed her eyes "I don't know, but don't worry, girls. I'm sure it's just a stupid prank. And we're going to find out who's behind it."

Everyone else looked relieved. They all went back to their rooms to get on with their day. Lexa, however, stayed behind. She winced as she looked over Ariana's hair.

"Wow. You got it the worst, huh?" she said.

"I guess so," Ariana replied, inwardly seething.

"Don't worry. Go shower and then I'll help you fix it up," Lexa offered with a smile.

"Thanks, Lexa," Ariana said, touched.

Safely inside her room, she picked up the jewelry box from the floor and placed it carefully on Kaitlynn's desk. Her hands were still shaking, but her pulse had slowed to normal. More than anything, she was annoyed that she had allowed herself to feel even a smidgen of fear over something that bitch had done.

For just a moment, Ariana had let Kaitlynn take control. She would not let it happen again.

SUPER SPIES

"Mr. Pitt?"

Ariana peaked through the open door of her guidance counselor's office. He was kicked back in his leather chair, eating a powdered-sugar donut and reading a well-worn copy of *A Brief History of Time*. The moment she appeared he sat up straight and coughed, puffing a cloud of white sugar all over his dark blue sweater-vest. Ariana did her best not to wrinkle her nose in disgust. She liked Mr. Pitt, but if he didn't want to be caught slacking-off while indulging in sugar-caked carbs, why leave the door open? This was basic stuff.

"Miss Covington!"

He slapped the book closed, dropped the donut onto a piece of waxed paper, and dusted off his desk with the pinky side of his hand. His gaze was expectant as he rested his thick forearms atop the clutter of his desk.

"Can I talk to you for a sec?" Ariana asked.

As she stepped inside, her hands clutched the strap on her messenger bag. Ever since the hair incident that morning, she'd been clenching her fists or clutching something all the time. She'd been forced to cut her extensions before she even got to Lexa so that her friend wouldn't realize her hair was fake. Then Lexa had shaped it into a new, shorter do that looked pretty shoddy, even though everyone kept telling her it was very *now*. As soon as she had a free minute she was going into town to get a real haircut.

"Absolutely." He gestured at the chair across from his desk, but she didn't take it. "What can I do for you?"

"I was wondering if you had any SAT study guides you could lend me," Ariana said. "I've decided to take the test in October so I'll have plenty of chances to try again."

Although she didn't actually feel the need for study guides, her plan of attack was factual. It was one of the awful drawbacks of starting over—having to retake the SATs. Three years ago she'd nailed a nearly perfect score, but she'd gotten it as Ariana Osgood. It meant nothing now. As much as Ariana had always enjoyed taking standardized tests—the tiny circles to fill in with perfectly sharpened pencils, the warm vibe of tension and fear permeating the air, the excitement of knowing the answer—she dreaded the idea that she might not be able to improve on her original score.

"Of course, of course." Mr. Pitt got up and wiped his fingers on his brown pants, leaving a white sugar streak on his thigh, which he failed to notice. He bent and yanked open the bottom drawer of the filing cabinet behind his desk, which made a loud squeal, as if it hadn't been pried free in decades. Ariana glanced over her shoulder at the door just as Brigit popped through.

"Mr. Pitt! The copier's jammed again," she said breathlessly. "I wouldn't bother you but I need to make copies of this flyer for the first French club meeting before my next class."

Mr. Pitt whirled around, slamming his ankle against the side of the open drawer. Both Ariana and Brigit winced as his face screwed up in pain.

"All right. I'll be right there," he said through his teeth, clearly trying to hold back a groan.

"Thanks!" Brigit said brightly. She didn't so much as glance at Ariana, which surprised her. Ariana had pegged Brigit as the type of coconspirator who wouldn't be able to resist a gleeful glance to acknowledge a plan going well. Ariana was impressed that Brigit had more self-control than that.

"With all the money pouring into this school you'd think that some small percentage could be allotted to updating the guidance office technology," Mr. Pitt muttered, limping around his desk. "Forgive me, Miss Covington. I should be back in a moment."

"Take your time," Ariana said with a smile. *All the time you need.*

The moment Mr. Pitt was gone, Ariana raced around his desk, sliding past the open drawer. She was about to drop into his chair, but then she noticed all the stains and crumbs and tears and decided to remain standing. He was already logged into the school's intranet, so when she typed Allison's name into the search box, her file popped right up. Moving purposefully, Ariana clicked open Allison's schedule and memorized it with one glance. She then opened her final report card from the previous year and smiled.

Allison was a straight-B student, except for one subject. In chemistry, she had received a D for the year. Which would account for the fact that she was taking it again this year. All Ariana had to do was write up a cheat sheet for Allison's first chemistry exam, plant it on the girl, and then make sure it was found. Easy as apple pie. She quickly closed the file and glanced at the open door. The hallway was quiet. No voices, no footfalls. Ariana's heart skipped an excited beat. There was one other person she was curious about, and she might not have an opportunity this golden again. She placed her fingers over the keyboard and typed in Palmer's name.

His schedule popped up. All AP courses, plus college-level electives in government and business. Ariana grinned. She'd known he was ambitious, just like herself. And his grades from last year were straight A's. Another file titled College Applications was just too tempting to resist. Ariana double clicked it and scanned the list of schools to which Palmer was planning to apply. Harvard, Yale, Cornell, Columbia, Arizona State (she supposed the son of the local congresswoman couldn't ignore his home state), and Princeton.

Princeton. The school Ariana planned to attend. Suddenly she saw the two of them strolling along cobblestone paths on a gorgeous autumn day, their feet crunching through the fallen leaves as they discussed politics and poetry and their plans for the future. It was all so perfect it hurt.

"Not a problem, Miss Rhygsted!"

Ariana's heart vaulted into her throat. Mr. Pitt's voice was right outside the door. She grabbed the mouse and closed Palmer's file. Then she whirled around and hit the floor next to the still-open cabinet drawer. She squeezed her eyes closed and held her breath. She could not get caught. Could not get expelled because of this. If she did, she was going to come back here and kill Kaitlynn. Kill her using the most gruesome, agonizing method she could devise. After all, if Atherton-Pryce was taken away from her, if Palmer and Lexa and Stone and Grave and the rest of her friends were torn away, if her new picture of her future was obliterated, she'd have nothing left to lose.

"Miss Covington?" Mr. Pitt said.

Ariana's eyes popped open. Right in front of her was the yellow and red spine of an SAT study guide, smiling up at her from the open drawer. Ariana grabbed it and stood.

"Oh, hi! Sorry. Class is going to start any minute so I figured I'd just grab one myself." She held the book up a bit higher to illustrate. "I hope you don't mind."

Mr. Pitt stood in the doorway for a moment. His eyes traveled slowly to his computer, then back to her. Ariana's pulse throbbed frantically. Was he going to call her out? Check his computer's history?

Please, no. Please, please, no.

But then he smiled. "Not at all. Anything to help a Princeton hopeful."

"Thank you," Ariana said with a smile. She kicked the drawer shut and walked around the desk, slipping by him out the door. The cover of the book was slick with her sweat.

Completely disgusting.

"Anytime!" he called after her.

As she walked down the hallway, Ariana's back was stiff, just waiting for him to yell after her again. For him to discover that she'd searched his computer. But all she heard was the squeal of his chair as he sat down again, and soon she was out the door, basking in the late-summer sunshine.

She slipped the book into her bag and withdrew a tissue on which to wipe her palms. Who was she kidding? The guy had probably gone right back to his donut.

"Hey!"

Brigit jogged up from behind a maple tree and joined Ariana, her many plastic bracelets doing a noisy dance.

"Well? Did you get what we need?" she whispered.

"Got it," Ariana said with a grin, glancing around the circle casually.

"Yes!" Brigit cheered under her breath. "I felt like a superspy or something. So what's next?"

"All I need is a sample of Allison's handwriting," Ariana replied coolly.

"You think you can copy it?" Brigit asked.

"I know I can," Ariana replied. "Remember that time you asked what my *thing* was?"

"Yeah," Brigit said excitedly.

"Well, it's forgery," Ariana said with a smirk.

"Sweet," Brigit replied, completely unscandalized. "I bet that will come in handy once we get into . . . you know."

Ariana's step lightened. She hadn't thought of that. "I bet it will."

"I'll get you something of Allison's," Brigit said confidently.

"Thanks, Brigit," Ariana said, nudging her in a friendly way. "I knew I could count on you."

Brigit smiled happily. "Oh, hey. There's Lillian!" she said, waving Kaitlynn down.

Ariana scowled as her roommate approached. She hadn't seen Kaitlynn since she'd woken up to the girl's surprise gift that morning.

"Hey, ladies," Kaitlynn greeted them. "Brigit, I *love* that necklace," she said. "Where'd you get it?"

Suck-up, Ariana thought.

"Thanks. It's a family heirloom," Brigit said, fingering the gold, diamonds, and aquamarines at her throat.

"So pretty," Kaitlynn replied. Then she looked at Ariana, her eyes dancing. "Nice haircut, A," she said. "I heard a few people got their hair chopped. Bizarre, huh?"

"Yeah. Bizarre," Ariana replied flatly. "You're *so* lucky they didn't get you."

"Yeah. I guess so," Kaitlynn tilted her head to the side, pretending to study the cut. "Maybe I can help you shape it later. I know a little something about short hair." She tossed her head to punctuate her point.

"Gee. Thanks. I bet you're good with scissors," Ariana replied.

"Oh, I am," Kaitlynn said. "Well, see you guys later. I just found out I placed into honors Spanish, so I have to get to the bookstore before lunch."

She twiddled her fingers and practically pranced away.

"See? That was sweet of her. She's making an effort," Brigit said.

Ariana clenched her teeth. "Yeah. Really sweet."

Sweet enough to make a girl barf.

THE SETUP

"Looks like you were right about your roommate," Soomie said as she and Ariana took their seats in the dining hall that day at lunch. Ariana followed her gaze and saw Kaitlynn settling into a chair at Tahira's table, laughing over something Zuri was saying. Ariana bit her tongue. Kaitlynn was no idiot. Psychotic, yes, but not an idiot. So what the hell was she doing with Tahira? If she wanted to be invited to the NoBash, she should have been sucking up to Brigit like she had earlier and avoiding Tahira like the latest strain of exotic flu. Or had it escaped her attention that there was a Princess War going on at Atherton-Pryce?

"Girl has no taste," Maria said under her breath, joining them.

"She's just trying to make friends," Ariana said, the words tasting like sawdust on her tongue. But if she was going to secure an invite to the NoBash for Kaitlynn, she had to talk her up.

Lexa strolled through the back entrance to the dining hall, her head bent in conversation with a petite girl with kinky red hair and glasses. Ariana had seen her around Wolcott Hall but had never met her. She was pretty in an unassuming way and wore no accessories other than an ancient, man's watch.

"Who's that with Lexa?" Ariana asked as the waiter approached their table.

"That would be April Corrigan," Soomie replied. "Résumé as follows: senior, first in her class for three straight years; president of APH's Amnesty International club, the APH Beautification Society, and the National Honor Society; editor of the *Weekly Report*, editor of *The Ash*, and captain of the women's lacrosse team."

"Wow. That's a serious overachiever," Ariana said, duly impressed.

The *Weekly Report* was the online student newspaper, and *The Ash* was the literary magazine, which published four times a year and had been the first publication to carry the work of at least half a dozen Nobel Laureates and national poetry award winners. She hoped to join the staff of *The Ash* herself, when they first met early next week. She hadn't written anything in a long time—not since Dr. Meloni had maligned her work in their sessions—but that didn't mean she couldn't critique other people's work.

"Maybe. Or maybe she's just unfocused," Soomie groused.

"Girl like that has no idea what she wants to do with her life," Maria agreed, sliding into her chair.

"Unlike our little Maria here, who wants to save the world with her powers of dance," Landon Jacobs put in, giving Maria a cheek pinch as he joined them.

"Says the boy who wants to save it through the power of pop," Maria said acerbically, barely making eye contact with her secret boyfriend.

"Hi, Landon!" Soomie said, sitting across from him.

Adam and Brigit walked in together and sat next to Soomie, so wrapped up in conversation they didn't even bother to greet anyone. Lexa split off from April and joined them just as the waiter arrived.

"What's up with April?" Soomie asked. "Starting another new club?"

"No, nothing like that," Lexa said with a brief smile.

Ariana saw Lexa, Maria, and Soomie exchange a quick glance. A casual observer wouldn't have caught it, but Ariana did, and her blood sizzled. Did April have something to do with Stone and Grave? Maybe she and Lexa were working together to figure out who had executed the prank that morning. Ariana wondered what they would do if they found Kaitlynn out. Disqualify her, probably. Could Ariana find a way to turn her in without Kaitlynn knowing?

For a moment, she felt the exhilaration of a new plan forming. But then reality set in. If Kaitlynn didn't get into Stone and Grave, Ariana would be the one to pay.

"What can I get everyone today?" the waiter asked, pencil at the ready.

Ariana ordered the turkey burger, seasoned fries, and a side salad. All this plotting and planning was making her hungry. Her friends quickly placed their orders as well and handed over their menus. The waiter was just about to step away from their table, from which Palmer was again absent, when Conrad Royce strode up and filled the vacant chair with his athletic bulk.

"Hey," he said to Ariana with a smile.

Ariana glanced at Lexa, who appeared bemused, then smiled at Conrad. "Hi. Glad you can join us. You know everyone, right?"

"Of course," Conrad said, dropping his burlap bag on the floor next to his chair. He leaned across the table to slap hands with Landon. "How's it going, bro? Heard you left a trail of broken hearts across Europe this summer. "

Maria blushed and looked down at her iPod, letting her hair hide her face. Had Landon really cheated on her, or was this just celebrity gossip?

Landon meanwhile, smiled, tossing his bangs back from his face. "You know how it is, man."

Conrad laughed. "Unfortunately, I don't." He shrugged out of his blue blazer and settled in. "Hey, Lexa," he said with a smile. "Saw you running the trail this morning. New kicks?"

Lexa smiled. "Yeah. This year's Asics line is so lightweight. Have you tried them?"

"Not yet, but if you think it's worth it, I will," he said with a smile.

Lexa blushed slightly and ran her hand under her hair at the nape of her neck, fluffing it out slightly. Ariana exchanged a triumphant look with her friends. She had chosen wisely.

The door to the dining hall opened and in walked Palmer. Ariana was surprised to see him, since he'd been spending all his meal hours in the Hill since he and Lexa had broken up. Was it just a coincidence that he'd chosen today to show up in the dining hall, or was he here to see whom Ariana had set Lexa up with? Apparently it was going to take a little bit more than random meetings in theaters and bathrooms to help Palmer forget his ex entirely.

Palmer was just turning his steps toward their table when he noticed that it was full—that Conrad was the guy who had taken his place. He hesitated a moment, then turned quickly and joined his friends from the crew team a few tables over.

"What can I get you, Mr. Royce?" the waiter asked.

Conrad placed his order and Ariana sat back in her chair. On her side of the table, Brigit and Adam flirted shamelessly, while across from her Lexa kept sliding glances at their handsome newcomer. Now if only she could find someone other than Landon for Soomie, maybe they could all be happily paired off before the NoBash.

Ariana looked over at Palmer to see how he was faring, seeing Lexa with another guy. Palmer looked right into her eyes, smiled broadly, and flashed her a discreet thumbs-up. Ariana's heart tingled with delight. So he wasn't jealous. He had just wanted to make sure Ariana had picked the right guy for Lexa. And apparently, he agreed that she had. Ariana couldn't have stopped grinning if she'd tried.

Yes, very soon they would *all* be happily paired up.

ACTION

Friday morning, Ariana awoke to find another pink jewelry box at her bedside, this one the perfect size for a ring. Her stomach filled with acidic dread. What had Kaitlynn done now?

Quaking from head to foot, Ariana got up and inspected her hair in the mirror. It looked the same. Badly cut, slightly matted from sleep. The same. She turned and stared at the jewelry box.

Don't open it. Don't play into her game. Ignore it.

She started for the bathroom, but just couldn't do it. The curiosity was too much. Cursing under her breath at her own weakness, she walked over and pried open the box. The contents tumbled out onto the floor, tiny little crescent moons, bouncing off in various directions. A lump formed in Ariana's throat as she realized she was looking at fingernails. Perfect clippings of fingernails. She turned her hands over. Her expert manicure was gone.

As her vision clouded, Ariana stumbled back and sat on her bed.

The box dropped, and out popped another folded slip of paper. Ariana could only imagine that it was another calendar—another countdown. Eight days left. She put her head between her knees and breathed.

In, one . . . two . . . three . . .

Out, one . . . two . . . three . . .

In, one . . . two . . . three . . .

Out, one . . . two . . . three . . .

How had she done it? How had she managed to lift Ariana's hands and cut her nails without waking her up? Ariana's stomach heaved.

She jumped up, dropping the box, and ran for the bathroom. As she retched over the toilet bowl, one thought kept repeating itself in her mind.

She's going to kill me. First she's torturing me, and then she's going to kill me.

Finally, Ariana lifted her head. She reached one shaking hand for the handle and flushed. Her butt on the cold ceramic floor, she drew the back of her hand across her mouth and hugged her knees to her chest.

Out in the hallway, Brigit shouted, then Tahira screamed, and Ariana knew that Kaitlynn had hit the others again, just for good measure. But little did they know that all of this was for Ariana's benefit. All of it engineered to remind her just how crazy and capable Kaitlynn was.

This week had gotten away from her what with class and the Allison plan and the Lexa and Conrad thing and everything else. But she couldn't put off safeguarding herself any longer.

It was time to take action.

INSURANCE

That morning, Ariana did the unthinkable: She skipped English class. As her cab pulled up to the covered front doorway of Wolcott Hall, she felt as if she was being watched. As if at any moment Headmaster Jansen was going to jump out from behind a potted plant and slap her with some kind of demerit. But it wasn't her fault. Circumstances were forcing her to break the rules. Right then, Kaitlynn was sequestered somewhere, taking her final placement test of the week, and it was the only time Ariana could be sure that the girl would not be able to follow her.

She got into the back of the cab, swallowed back her guilt-induced nausea, and gave the driver the address she'd printed off the Internet.

You're skipping for a reason, she told herself. *A very important reason. It's just one class and you can always get the notes from someone.*

From Conrad.

Her skin tingled as the idea occurred to her. It was perfect, actually.

She could use her transgression as an excuse for throwing Conrad and Lexa together again. She might have been committing a crime against academia, but at least she could make something good come out of it. The thought comforted her, eased her racing pulse, and she sat back against the vinyl seat, feeling much more relaxed.

Twenty minutes later, the cab pulled up in front of stately white columns of the First American Bank. Ariana paid the driver, got out of the car, and walked purposefully up the stone stairs. The guard at the door eyed her disinterestedly as she strolled past the tellers and right up to the information desk. The elderly gentleman behind the counter looked up at her and smiled. His teeth were yellow, but his white hair was perfectly coiffed and his brown eyes alert. His burgundy wing tips, Ariana noted, were freshly buffed, and his gold name tag read BERNARD.

"Can I help you?"

"Yes. I'd like to rent a safety-deposit box," Ariana said confidently. Sometimes older men saw a teenage girl and refused to take her seriously. Ariana found that an authoritative tone could often preclude a lot of patronizing talk.

"I can assist you with that," he said. He opened a slim drawer and pulled out a white card. "You'll need to fill this out and sign at the bottom, and then I'll just need to see an ID."

Ariana quickly filled out the card with all her information and signed Briana Leigh's name at the bottom. She placed the pen down and removed her Texas driver's license from her wallet. Bernard slipped the card from the counter to inspect it and held the license up against the signature. Ariana snapped her bag closed and waited.

And waited. And waited. The man stared at the signatures, looked up at Ariana's face, narrowed his eyes. Ariana's heart started to pound.

She told herself to relax. The man was just doing his job, that was all. It was Ariana in the picture. Ariana's Briana Leigh signature on both documents. There was no reason for him to suspect anything.

Then Bernard reached for the phone on his desk. Ariana stopped breathing. He was calling security. Ariana surreptitiously looked over her shoulder at the door, wondering how fast the security guard could possibly be. Wondering if she was faster.

Bernard picked up his glasses, which were resting on the counter next to the phone, and slipped them on.

"I apologize," he said with a chuckle. "I keep telling myself I don't need them, but obviously I do."

Ariana let out a breath, relief flooding her body like a cool drink. Bernard was simply blind as a bat. Seconds later he handed back her ID and got up from his stool.

"This way, Miss Covington."

Her knees trembled—a lingering side effect of the abject fear—as she followed him across the gleaming red stone floor and into a small room outside the deposit box area.

"Wait here, please."

She did as she was told, falling into the wooden chair at the tiny counter with relief.

"All right, you'll have box number 167," Bernard said, returning with a long silver tray covered by a sliding top. "Here are your keys."

He placed two bronze keys on the desk in front of her with a clang. "You can place your items inside, and when you're finished, use that phone to signal me," he said, pointing at an old-fashioned white phone on the wall. "We'll go in and replace the box and lock it together."

"Understood," Ariana said with a nod.

"Take your time."

Bernard smiled and left her alone. Ariana took a deep breath and removed the items she needed from her bag. One piece of thick parchment paper, one Cross pen, one envelope. Glancing over her shoulder to ensure she was completely alone, Ariana got to work. In her own hand, she wrote out a brief version of her story. How she'd broken out of the Brenda T. How she'd murdered Briana Leigh Covington to assume her identity and to provide the authorities with a body to cremate in her place. How Kaitlynn had been released at her bidding as well. And how, if someone was reading this, it meant she was dead. And if she was dead, Kaitlynn had murdered her. She provided details of Kaitlynn's whereabouts, of her new name, of the one other fake name she had used since escaping. She then slipped a photo from her purse, one she had taken with her phone and printed out that morning. A photo of Kaitlynn sleeping in her bed so that anyone who read this note would know what Kaitlynn looked like today. Different hair, different name, different style—same sociopath. She signed the letter with a name she hadn't used in months.

Sincerely,
Ariana Osgood

She folded the letter, placed it in the envelope along with the photo, and sealed it. Then she summoned Bernard. Together they replaced the box among the hundreds of others inside the cold, airy vault. Ariana used her key to lock her lock, then Bernard used the bank's key to lock the second.

There it was. Her life's secret. Hidden in a nondescript row of nondescript boxes in the middle of one of thousands of banks in the Washington, D.C., area. Safe. Until she was dead.

"No one will be able to open this box without both keys," Bernard explained. "Is there anything else I can do for you, Miss Covington?"

"No, thank you," Ariana replied, slipping her two copies of her key into her bag. She was surprised to find her fingers were trembling and took a breath to steady herself. "I appreciate all your help."

"Of course," he said as he led her out of the room and secured the vault door behind them. "Have a nice day, Miss Covington."

Oh, I will, Ariana thought as she traipsed out of the bank and hailed another cab, this time bound for the nearest upscale salon. Why not indulge in a new haircut? It was time to celebrate. She had just bought her life insurance plan. If Kaitlynn hurt her, she wouldn't get away with it. Now all she had to do was send the extra key to Briana Leigh's trusted personal maid in Texas, with the instructions to go and open the box and read the letter if anything should happen to Briana Leigh. And tell Kaitlynn what she'd done, of course. That was the point of all this—to let Kaitlynn know that if Ariana died, Kaitlynn was sure to be arrested.

It was the perfect plan. Nothing could harm her now.

UP IN SMOKE

Kaitlynn hummed Tchaikovsky's *Swan Lake* as she got ready for bed that evening, spreading moisturizer over her arms and legs, filing her nails, combing her hair. Ariana sat on her bed with her phone, tossed her now perfectly shaped, chin-length hair, and texted Conrad.

Borrow ur English notes?

The reply was instant.

sure meet tmrw?

Ariana grinned and texted back.

After bkfst @ pond?

Conrad replied with one word.

done

Ariana slipped her phone back into her bag and got up to turn down her bed, feeling satisfied. It was all about taking one thing at a time, planning, plotting, staying positive.

"What are you so happy about, A?" Kaitlynn asked.

Just the sound of the girl's voice put a damper on Ariana's triumph. Suddenly all she could think about was what Kaitlynn was planning for that night. Was she going to double-pierce Ariana's ears? Pull out all her eyelashes? Every muscle in her body tensed at the thought of someone else trying to control her emotions, her life, her fate.

"Well, *Lillian*," Ariana began, turning to face her nemesis. It was time to regain control. "There's something I've been meaning to tell you."

"Oh, yeah?" Kaitlynn asked, perching on the edge of her bed.

"I've taken out a safety-deposit box," Ariana said. Kaitlynn's eyebrows arched with interest. "In it is a letter describing every single thing you and I have been through stating that if anything should happen to me, you're the one who did it. I've sent the key to someone I trust, along with a letter telling that person where the box is and to open it if I turn up dead."

Kaitlynn blinked. She betrayed not one iota of emotion. She simply blinked.

"So you can threaten me all you want, but you don't scare

me," Ariana continued. "If I die, you're getting the chair. Are we clear?"

Kaitlynn started to hum again. She got up, walked into her closet, and rummaged around. Ariana held her breath. Her heart pounded wildly in her chest. What was Kaitlynn doing? Looking for some kind of weapon? Did she have a gun in there or something? Hadn't she heard a word Ariana had just said? Quickly, Ariana glanced around for something with which to defend herself. Her eyes fell on her tennis racket. It was all she had. She was just lunging for it when Kaitlynn emerged with a long, cream-colored envelope.

"You mean this letter?" she asked, tossing it on Ariana's bed.

Ariana's pulse froze in her veins. Both the letter and the picture of Kaitlynn had slipped free of the torn envelope when they'd hit her bedspread. This was not possible.

"How . . . how did you . . . ?"

"I followed you, Ariana," Kaitlynn said flatly. "When I saw you get into that cab instead of scurrying off to class like the responsible little student you are, I knew something was up, so I followed you. After I figured out what you were doing at the bank, I followed you to the salon and lifted your key and ID while you were getting shampooed."

Ariana grabbed her bag from her desk chair and yanked out her wallet. Sure enough, the key and her license were gone. How could she not have noticed it before?

"Then I went back to the bank, waited for that geezer to get off duty, forged Briana Leigh's signature, and emptied the box."

"But didn't they . . . you don't look anything like my picture," Ariana said breathlessly.

"The guy barely even glanced at it. I had the key and the signature. Besides, he was too busy checking out my ass."

She removed Ariana's license from her top dresser drawer and Frisbeed it at Ariana. It fell to the floor at their feet. Ariana could think of nothing to say. Once again, Kaitlynn had won.

"Thanks a lot, Ariana," Kaitlynn continued. "Because of you I have to spend my Saturday afternoon taking the final placement exam I missed. You're really screwing me up around here, you know that?"

No, you're screwing me *up and we both know it,* Ariana thought.

Kaitlynn took a deep breath and blew out a sigh. "It was a nice try," she said, grabbing up the envelope, along with its former contents. "But I think I'd better burn this now, don't you?"

With a tilt of her head, Kaitlynn turned, walked into the bathroom, and slammed the door behind her. Ariana heard the strike of the match, but didn't wait to smell the smoke. Feeling numb, she grabbed a pillow off her bed, slipped the comforter free, and walked out the door with them. If she stayed in her own room any longer, she knew the sense of helplessness hovering just outside her protective wall would come smashing through and take over. And she could not have that. Could not give up. There was too much at stake. Down the hall she knocked on Lexa and Maria's door. Maria answered, her hair up in a messy bun, her toothbrush sticking out of her mouth. Her cropped black T-shirt exposed one tanned strip of perfectly flat stomach.

"She's on the phone with Conrad," Maria whispered conspiratorially, gesturing over her shoulder at Lexa.

Ariana forced a smile. "That's great. Listen, can I sleep in your lounge tonight?"

"Sure," Maria said, opening the door wide. "What's up? Problems with Lily?"

A lump formed in Ariana's throat. How she wished she could tell the truth, confide in her friend, pour it all out to her. But it was all going to have to stay bottled up in her chest, churning and bubbling and threatening to explode in the form of desperate tears.

Why couldn't she get anything right lately? Why did it seem as if Kaitlynn was always one step ahead?

"No. She has some allergy issues and she's been snoring a lot. After a whole week of listening to it, I just want one good night's sleep," Ariana said.

"I hear ya. Lexa snores too," Maria said.

"I do not!" Lexa cried from her bed. She gave Ariana a wave and went back to her conversation.

"Want to hang out? We were going to watch *Real Housewives* on my laptop till lights-out," Maria offered, going back into the bathroom to rinse her mouth.

"No, thanks. I'm exhausted," Ariana said. "I'm just going to crash."

"Okay. G'night!" Maria said as Ariana opened the door to the lounge.

She dropped her pillow on the couch and settled in for what was sure to be an uncomfortable night's sleep. But it had to be better than sleeping next to Kaitlynn, listening to her laugh in her sleep, flinching at her every move. At least here she could concentrate on trying to plot her next move.

Even though she was sure that whatever she came up with, Kaitlynn was going to think of it first.

OUT OF CONTROL

"Oh my God! What the hell!?"

Ariana's eyes wrenched open and she sat up straight, her heart pounding in her throat. In the next room, Lexa was shouting at the top of her lungs. For a moment, Ariana clung to her comforter, trying to remember why she was on Maria and Lexa's couch. Then Maria screeched as if she'd just stepped on a rat.

Out of the corner of her eye Ariana spotted it. Another pink velvet ring box, sitting on the coffee table.

Ariana grabbed the box and pried it open: Out dropped two red crescent moons. She flung the comforter aside and checked her feet. Sure enough her big toenails had been cut to the quick. At that moment, Maria and Lexa burst into the room.

"She has one too!" Maria cried, rushing to Ariana's side, her half-fallen bun bouncing around atop her head. She looked down at the toenails on the floor and then jumped up on the couch behind Ariana as if she were afraid they were going to bite. "Omigod, omigod. Who would *do* this?" she cried, hugging herself.

Ariana glanced at Maria's toes, which were all gnarly and blistered from being shoved into her pointe shoes every day of her life. Just like Ariana's, her big toenails were freshly shorn.

"You know what, girls? I think I've finally figured it out," Lexa said calmly, placing her own empty box on the bookshelf near the door. She crossed her arms over her red silk pajama top.

"You have?"

Ariana's throat constricted so quickly it hurt. She clutched the pink box in both hands. If either Maria or Lexa decided to inspect it more closely, they were sure to find the countdown calendar that was certain to be tucked inside.

Seven more days . . .

"Omigod! You guys have them, too?" Kaitlynn appeared in the doorway, holding a pink box in her hands. Ariana's face burned with anger at the very sight of her. She, Lexa, and Maria all looked down at Kaitlynn's feet, where her big toenails had been jaggedly clipped.

All the better to throw them off her scent. Brilliant.

Ariana took a deep breath. "Lexa was just about to tell us who she thinks is doing this." She turned the pink box over and over in her hands, hating that she had to act as Kaitlynn's accomplice, even as she was one of her victims.

"Who?" Kaitlynn didn't miss a beat. She walked in and sat down on the couch, looking up at Lexa like a lost child. Maria perched on the armrest.

"Well, by now I'm sure you all know there are a few secret societies here at Atherton-Pryce," Lexa began.

She gave Ariana a no-nonsense look and Ariana got her meaning immediately. She wasn't to mention the fact that Lexa had told her about the secret societies during Welcome Week. It was such an odd game they were all playing. If Maria and Lexa were both in Stone and Grave, as Ariana suspected, they both knew she and Kaitlynn had already been tapped. Yet none of them was allowed to acknowledge what they knew about the others.

"Well, this has the Fellows written all over it," Lexa said.

"The Fellows?" Ariana asked, sitting down next to Kaitlynn. Her legs felt as if she had run a mile. It was hard to believe that three minutes ago she had been dead asleep.

"Definitely," Maria said with a nod. "Those guys can be seriously morbid."

And dragging people up to the woods with bags over their heads to a fire surrounded by human skulls is what? Whimsical? Ariana thought.

"Someone is going to have to retaliate," Lexa said with a mischievous glint in her eye.

"Oh, yes. Someone definitely should," Maria agreed.

Ariana just let them talk, wondering if Kaitlynn knew how dangerous this whole game was. If Lexa or anyone else had started to suspect Kaitlynn, there was no way Ariana would have been able to convince them to accept her. There was no way Brigit was going to invite a midnight toenail clipper to the NoBash. Kaitlynn would get none of the things she wanted, and would undoubtedly blame it on Ariana.

Somehow twist it so that Ariana's delay in sabotaging someone had forced her to do what she'd done.

Kaitlynn was much more than off the deep end; she was being pulled out to sea by a strong undertow. Ariana was not dealing with a person who could be reasoned with, a person whose moves could be predicted. Kaitlynn was out of control.

And that scared Ariana more than anything.

COUPLES, COUPLES, COUPLES

At least it was a beautiful day. Hot and sunny with a light breeze. The perfect day for lazing around by the pond, pretending to study and working on one's tan. Which made it easy to convince Lexa and the others to join her down by the water after breakfast. As Ariana lay on her stomach atop a crisp cotton blanket, her copy of Kate Chopin's *The Awakening* open in front of her, she breathed deeply and tried not to think about Kaitlynn and her psychosis. She had to focus on the positive. And right now, the Lexa-and-Conrad plan was going perfectly. Soon after she and her friends had settled in, Conrad had arrived with his English notes as scheduled and quickly fallen into conversation with Lexa. The pair was currently strolling around the water's edge, pausing every now and then to admire the flower beds or watch the pair of swans cutting their graceful arcs across the pond's surface.

They were obviously smitten. Ariana was sure that Lexa would ask Conrad to the NoBash any day now. Then she could officially be declared over Palmer and he would be free to escort someone else to the party. Namely, Ariana. Sometimes she just couldn't get over her own brilliance.

"Anyone thirsty?" Soomie asked, looking up from her thick physics text. "I'm gonna text Melanie and ask her to bring down some iced tea and snacks."

"Lemonade for me, please," Ariana said, pushing her sunglasses atop her head.

"Iced tea works for us," Brigit put in. "Us" meaning herself and Adam, who hadn't left her side all day. The two of them were currently sharing a pair of earbuds attached to Brigit's pink iPod, sitting so close together on their picnic blanket that Brigit's knee rested atop his thigh. So much for Brigit's nervousness around boys.

"Wait. You're texting who for what now?" Adam asked, brushing aside a pesky bee that had been hovering for the last few minutes.

"It's a long story. Brigit will fill you in," Soomie said, her thumbs already flicking over the keys.

Ariana smiled as Brigit started to explain the whole concept of the sophomore slaves to Adam, trying not to make it sound scandalous, which it easily could. They really did make a cute couple. She glanced at Soomie, wondering what sort of guy she would like if she didn't have a crush on Landon. Maria had begged off the study session, saying that she had a pointe class in the city, while Landon was supposedly doing some interview for *Entertainment Weekly*. Ariana had a hunch that they'd sneaked off together for some alone time. While she fully respected Maria's right to a secret relationship, she felt bad for Soomie, lusting after a guy who was seeing one of her best friends.

She was about to return to her book and save the Soomie dilemma for another time when Kaitlynn's familiar laugh caught her attention. Ariana had avoided having to even look at her at breakfast by sitting with her back to Tahira's table. Now her shoulders curled as she glanced at the shoreline, flicking over the various groups of students dotted here and there. When she found the girl, she froze. Kaitlynn was standing near the edge of the pond in a pair of barely there shorts, chatting with Palmer Liriano.

Ariana's vision instantly clouded over with tiny gray dots. She tried to breathe, but her throat closed in on her like a trapdoor.

What were Kaitlynn and Palmer doing together? How did they even know each other?

"What do you think of Lillian, Ana?" Soomie asked, following her gaze. "You live with her. Got any good dirt?"

She's a bitch. An evil, sadistic, conniving, completely insane bitch who cuts off people's body parts in the middle of the night. How's that for dirt?

But she couldn't say that. Of course she couldn't. At breakfast, Lexa and Maria had told everyone their theory, and they all had agreed that the Fellows were the most likely culprits. On the way out of the dining hall, Maria and Christian had cornered Palmer, who was eating all his meals with the crew team, and Ariana had a feeling they were confabbing about how to get back at the other society. Kaitlynn was in the clear, she knew.

"Ana?"

In, one . . . two . . . three . . .
Out, one . . . two . . . three . . .
In, one . . . two . . . three . . .
Out, one . . . two . . . three . . .

Not only could she not tell the truth about Kaitlynn, but she had to talk her up. Had to get her an invitation to the NoBash. With Kaitlynn threatening murder at every turn, Ariana wasn't about to take chances. She would not allow herself be killed over something as trifling as a party invite.

"She's pretty cool," Ariana said finally, feeling as if she was going to vomit or faint or both. "Actually, I was going to ask you, Brigit," Ariana said, looking over her shoulder. "Do you have any invites left for the NoBash?"

Brigit tore her eyes away from Adam's cute face and glanced curiously over at Kaitlynn. "A couple. Why? Do you want me to invite her?"

Actually, I'd rather you tear out every strand of hair from my head one by one, Ariana thought.

"No. I mean, I wouldn't presume to tell you who to invite," Ariana said with a wave of her hand.

"But if you're friends with her . . ." Brigit said.

Ariana tasted bile in the back of her throat. "Don't invite her on my account. I mean, you should get to know her first so you can decide," she said, sitting up and crossing her legs. She placed her book aside with regret. "I know. Why don't I invite her on our shopping trip? She has to take her last placement exam, but maybe she can meet up with us afterward."

Brigit and Soomie looked over at Kaitlynn again. She and Palmer were looking over something in a notebook, their heads bent rather close together for Ariana's comfort.

"Okay," Brigit said. "It'd probably be good to get to know her."

"Definitely," Soomie added, starting another text.

Ariana guessed that Soomie was interested in evaluating Kaitlynn for Stone and Grave. Part of her wished Kaitlynn would do something stupid so Soomie would blackball her and this whole thing could be over. If Kaitlynn was kept out because of her own mistakes, she couldn't exactly take it out on Ariana.

Not that she wouldn't anyway. Logic wasn't a big motivating factor for the deranged.

"Good. It's a plan," Ariana said.

Then she replaced her sunglasses over her eyes and tilted her head back so that the sun could warm her face—and so she could monitor Kaitlynn and Palmer out of the corner of her eye.

SMOOTH

"Brigit! I just found the perfect shoes to go with your gown!" Lexa announced, jogging up to Brigit and Ariana, who stood before a brightly lit wall peppered with small, silver shelves, displaying the most gorgeous array of shoes Ariana had ever seen. Behind them, Soomie, Maria, and Kaitlynn were trying on pair after pair of Jimmy Choos and Manolos and Louboutins. Every time Kaitlynn spoke, Ariana's shoulders tensed, so she was trying to tune her out. At least she had been alone with Brigit and Lexa for the gown-shopping portion of the trip. The three of them had hit the shops fast and hard before meeting up with the others for the shoe hunt. In the third boutique they had stormed, Ariana had found the perfect light blue chiffon gown, which was now hanging behind the counter where the salesgirl had offered to keep it safe and crease free while Ariana and her friends shopped.

"Let me see!" Brigit replied, bright-eyed.

Lexa pulled her hands out from behind her back. Ariana breathed in awe at the silver shoes. They each had one tiny purple stone just to the side of the peep-toe—the exact same shade as Brigit's dress. Unfortunately, they also had three-and-a-half inch heels.

"You can wear them, since your toenails weren't destroyed by some lunatic in the middle of the night," Lexa said with a laugh.

Ariana glanced at Kaitlynn, who was sitting on a leather settee. Her lips twitched ever so slightly. Ariana narrowed her eyes. What had she and Palmer been talking about down by the pond? Did Kaitlynn somehow know about Ariana's thing with Palmer? It made sense, because if she did, then obviously she would go after him. The girl clearly wanted everything Ariana had.

"Lexa! I love them!" Brigit said with false excitement. Then she scowled. "Now put them back."

"But Brigit! Come on!" Lexa wheedled. "You have to wear heels sometime!"

"Wait, you don't wear heels?" Kaitlynn asked, looking up.

"Never have, never will," Brigit replied. "What's the big deal, anyway?"

"The big deal is you're a princess. Princesses wear heels," Kaitlynn replied, lifting a hand.

"Couldn't have put it better myself," Maria added, pointing her toe in a basic black Christian Louboutin stiletto.

"Besides, Brigit, look at all the beautiful shoes you're missing out on!" Soomie added, standing up and looking around, her palms up. "This place is roughly eighty-eight percent heels and only twelve percent flats."

"It's practically a crime against fashion that you're excluding all these poor, poor shoes," Lexa said, holding the silver shoe up in front of her face and pouting at Brigit over the toe. "Come on, if you don't get these I'm going to have to buy them out from under you. I need a new pair of shoes for my date with Conrad tonight."

"You're going out with Conrad tonight?" Ariana asked, practically breathless.

Lexa blushed. "He's taking me to the opera," she said giddily. "How sophisticated are we?"

Ariana grinned. Lexa was clearly smitten. It was all she could do to keep from laughing in happiness.

"Good. Then you buy them," Brigit said, waving at the shoe dismissively.

"No way. I was only kidding," Lexa said. "You have to try them on."

"Ana? Help me out here," Brigit implored.

Ariana looked around at her friends—everyone but Kaitlynn—their faces pleading.

"Why don't you just try them?" she suggested. "Let us see how bad the situation really is."

Brigit's shoulder's slumped. "Fine," she groused. "But if . . . no, *when* I break my leg, you guys are explaining it to my parents."

"Deal," Ana said.

"We need these in a six!" Lexa cried, corralling the nearest salesman before Brigit could change her mind.

Ten minutes later, Brigit was outfitted with the shoes. She sat on a leather chair and looked down at her feet.

"My feet have never been so dressed up in their lives," she said with a smile.

"They are absolutely gorgeous," Kaitlynn said, hovering over her.

Brigit looked hopefully up at her. "You think?" she asked, moving her feet from side to side to inspect them from every angle.

"Without a doubt," Kaitlynn replied with a friendly smile. Ariana did her best not to gag.

"Okay. But you might want to stay out of my way," Brigit warned. She raised her arms up to Lexa like a toddler asking to be picked up. Lexa clasped Brigit around her elbows and hoisted her from her seat. Immediately, Brigit's right ankle gave out. Her arms flailed, clipping Kaitlynn in the cheek, and she fell right back into her chair.

"Warned you," Brigit said moodily. Her face burned with frustration and embarrassment. "Sorry, Kaitlynn."

"It's fine. I'm fine. Don't give up on my account. You can do this, Brigit," Kaitlynn said, spreading it on a tad thick, in Ariana's opinion.

"Come on. Let's try it again," Ariana said, moving forward to help Brigit this time.

She tugged Brigit to her feet and together they walked slowly around the myriad shoe boxes and discarded heels to a more open area of the shop. Brigit picked her way along as if she were walking on tiptoe through a field of glass. Every few steps, her ankles wobbled as if they were made of marshmallow rather than bone and cartilage. But Ariana kept a firm grip on the girl, and they were able to traverse the store without anyone getting injured.

"See? You can totally do it!" Lexa cheered.

"Sure. As long as Adam doesn't mind being my personal walker all night long," Brigit said.

"Adam's your date?" Kaitlynn asked, her eyebrows arched. "Adam with the insanely long legs?"

"That's the one," Soomie replied.

"Well, then you have to get them. How are you going to dance with a guy who's nearly a foot taller than you without heels?" Kaitlynn asked.

Ariana shot her a look. Who was she to be telling Brigit what she needed? But the other girls just nodded.

"She's right, Bridge," Maria said. "You don't want him to be stooping all night."

Brigit sighed. "No. But I also don't feel like breaking my neck, either."

"That's not going to happen," Lexa said, putting a supportive hand on Brigit's arm. "Maria will work on it with you, right?"

"I can make you graceful by next week, guaranteed," Maria assured her.

"Besides, I've already seen Tahira's shoes and they look like Birkenstocks next to those little lovelies," Kaitlynn added.

Ariana's heart skipped a beat as Brigit looked up, her eyes hungry. Kaitlynn had just sealed the deal.

"Really? They're fugly?" she asked.

Kaitlynn laughed, her hand to her chest. "I wouldn't say fugly, but she will drool when she sees these."

Brigit dropped into her chair, kicked off the shoes, and put them back in the box. "Ring these up, would you?" she said, handing them to a passing salesman.

"My pleasure," he said.

Brigit shoved her feet into her sneakers and stood up again. "Thanks, guys. I never would have done this without you." She moved past them toward the counter. Ariana grabbed the shoes she'd chosen and went with her.

"Are you sure about this?" she asked. "I mean, those shoes are amazing, but I want you to be comfortable."

"I'll be fine," Brigit said. "You heard Maria. She's going to train me."

They stopped at the counter together and looked back at the four girls, who were mulling over a pair of knee-high boots Maria was considering.

"Kaitlynn's pretty cool, huh?" Brigit said, handing over her American Express Black. "I wasn't so sure about her, but she just totally gave me inside info on Tahira."

Ariana bit her tongue. She had been so involved with her other plans and plots that spying on Tahira had fallen by the wayside, and Kaitlynn had just swooped in and saved the day.

"Yeah, she's pretty cool," Ariana agreed nonchalantly.

And smooth, she thought as Kaitlynn threw her head back in a laugh at something Maria had said. *Very, very smooth.*

BACKUP PLAN

"Thanks for the invite, A, that was super fun," Kaitlynn said sarcastically as she closed their dorm room door behind them. She lifted her messenger bag over her head, tossed it on the floor, and dropped dramatically onto her bed, splaying her arms over her head. "That Lexa chick is just *way* too cheerleader. And Maria? Does she always walk with her nose that far in the air? What's she trying to do, catch flies in there? Brigit's about the only one of them I can stand."

Ariana's jaw clenched. She walked into her closet and shoved aside a few hangers to make room for her new light blue gown. Then she shoved aside some more simply to make noise and release her aggression.

"If you don't like them, why are you so determined to hang out with them? Why don't you just find yourself some other clique to invade?"

Kaitlynn laughed. "For the same reason you latched on to them, A. They're the best. Besides, you're always with them, and I do *so* cherish our quality time together," she added sarcastically.

Ariana clung to the clothing rail with both hands and leaned forward, stretching out the backs of her arms and holding in a groan.

Control, Ariana. Control. You cannot rip down this clothing bar and impale her with it.

Although the visual was comforting.

Ariana straightened up, sighed, and looked down at her feet. She could get through this. She could. Look how much she had survived already. She rolled her shoulders back and walked over to the doorway between her closet and her room. Narrowing her eyes, she leaned against the doorjamb and looked at the girl whom she'd once called her best friend.

"Well, you made some progress today," she said. "But if I were you, I'd quit hanging out with Tahira and the Shrill Brigade. In case you hadn't noticed, Brigit is not a big fan."

"I've noticed," Kaitlynn said, shoving herself off the bed and crossing to her dresser. She pulled out a short-sleeved black cashmere top with a wide neckline. Then she shimmied out of her shorts and stepped into a flimsy silver skirt. "But a girl has to have a backup plan."

She popped open her sickly sweet perfume and dabbed a bit onto her wrists and behind her ears.

"Besides, Tahira and Allison are probably going to be in Stone and Grave with me," she said, lifting a shoulder. "We're going to be friends anyway."

It didn't escape Ariana's attention that she had been left out of that equation. What Kaitlynn didn't know was that Allison was never going to get into Stone and Grave. Not if she had her way.

"The others are in already, aren't they?" Kaitlynn asked, glancing at Ariana in the mirror. "Every one of them but Brigit."

"I don't know," Ariana said.

"Oh, please." Kaitlynn's eyes danced. "You spend all that time with them and you don't know? Or maybe you just don't want to tell me because you're afraid of what I might do."

Ariana's hand closed around her forearm and squeezed. It was all she could do to keep from backhanding the girl across the cheek. Kaitlynn turned around to face her.

"Let me ask you this . . . if one of them *had* to die, which one would you prefer?" she asked, her eyes dancing merrily. "Soomie, I bet, right? The smarty-pants. It'd make it a lot easier for you to graduate number one in our class," she said, looking Ariana up and down derisively, as if wanting to be valedictorian was somehow lame.

"None of them is going to have to die," Ariana told Kaitlynn firmly. "I have the situation under control."

Kaitlynn smiled slowly. Her eyes took on a predatory gleam that made Ariana's blood run cold. "I do hope so, A. Otherwise things are going to get very messy around here."

As if things weren't already messy, what with the nails and the hair everywhere. But if all went as it should, it would be over by Monday afternoon.

Kaitlynn walked over to her closet, stepped into a pair of black pumps, and grabbed a clutch purse, which she stocked with lip gloss, an atomizer, and some cash.

"Tahira and Rob are setting me up with some guy from GW tonight. How do I look?" she asked.

"Like a poisonous snake," Ariana replied.

"Perfect," Kaitlynn replied.

There was a quick rap on the door and Tahira waltzed right in, wearing a high-necked, sleeveless dress in a horribly bright fuchsia.

"Let's get a move on, beyotch," she said fondly, double air-kissing Kaitlynn. "Don't want to keep the men waiting."

"Heaven forbid," Kaitlynn said with a laugh. Then she turned to Ariana and gave her a pointed smile. "How do I look?" she asked again. She was testing Ariana. Seeing if she would be rude to her in front of someone else. Seeing if Ariana would risk Kaitlynn's ire.

"Like a slutty beyotch," Ariana said with a grin, mimicking Tahira's tone. Tahira giggled, clearly taking Ariana's insult as a friendly joke. Kaitlynn's smile faltered, and Ariana cocked a triumphant brow.

After a moment Kaitlynn notched her smile back up to full wattage. "Thanks, A! Have a good night! Hope you don't get to bored sitting here twiddling your thumbs!"

She and Tahira both laughed, looping their arms together as they waltzed out. Ariana slammed the door behind them and clenched her fists, annoyed that Kaitlynn had managed to get the last laugh. But at least she had gotten the last slam.

That had to count for something.

VERY RIGHT

Saturday night. Saturday night and Ariana was sitting alone in her dorm room, staring out the window at the winking lights of the APH campus. Brigit was having dinner with Adam. Maria had gone out with some friends from the Washington Ballet. Soomie had tagged along with Landon to some awful-sounding album-signing thing in the city. Lexa was taking in the opera with Conrad. Even Kaitlynn was out on a date. Ariana should have been out on a date as well. But she couldn't be. Because the boy she liked was still Lexa's territory, and would be until Lexa and Conrad were officially together.

But was that even true? Ariana wondered. What was the appropriate hands-off time before a girl could move in on her friend's ex even if the girl had a new boyfriend? Were she and Palmer going to have to continue sneaking around until they were off at Princeton together?

Just thinking about Palmer made Ariana groan with longing. She crossed her arms on her desk and put her head down. This was so unfair. Why did she have to fall for Palmer, of all people? She wondered where he was right then. Was he out having fun as well? Or was he, perhaps, somewhere inside the dorm? Somewhere alone, thinking about her as well.

Every inch of Ariana's body tingled. Screw this. Lexa was out on a date, for God's sake. With an incredible, hot guy. She pushed herself up, got halfway to her door, then hesitated. Lexa would die if she found out about Ariana and Palmer. But she wanted to go find him so badly her fingertips hurt.

Lexa would just have to not find out.

Ariana opened the door and strode out into the hallway. She took the elevator down to the first floor, walked over to the Alpha tower elevator, and took it all the way back up to the top, where Palmer's room was located. Just yanking open the heavy door that separated the boys' rooms from their common area made her feel powerful and free. She heard the sound of raucous boy laughter coming from one of the rooms. A bunch of guys playing video games, no doubt. Ariana hoped Palmer wasn't with them. Drawing him away from a pack of guys would be awkward, not to mention very public.

She walked over to the closed door at the end of the hallway and knocked. Seconds later, it opened. Palmer stood there in a black T-shirt and gray shorts. He smiled.

"I thought you'd never get here."

He opened the door wider and Ariana slipped inside. "How did you know I was coming?"

"I didn't. But I was hoping," Palmer said.

Then he closed the door behind them. Ariana's heart caught.

"Isn't that against the rules?" she asked, her heart fluttering in her throat.

Palmer pulled her to him. His body felt hard and strong against hers. "Do you really care about the rules right now?" he asked gently.

Ariana just smiled.

"Yeah. That's what I figured," Palmer said.

And then his lips were on hers and she was lying back on his bed and he was tugging off her shirt and she was sliding her hands over his chest and the lights were off and the sheets were soft and his body was perfect and she knew this was right . . . and Ariana simply let go. Because right then, nothing else mattered.

Not Lexa, not Stone and Grave, not Kaitlynn, not her future, not anything.

Nothing, nothing, nothing . . . but how very right this was.

COMING TOGETHER

Ariana sat at her desk on Sunday morning with Allison's handwriting sample in front of her, meticulously re-creating the girl's slanty print in a new, clean notebook. Brigit had somehow managed to tear a page out of Allison's chem notebook, which was a stroke of genius. Without it, Ariana wouldn't have known that Allison slanted her "equals" signs down or that she used a small circle in place of an x when multiplying. Any other writing sample would have been useless.

Brigit was the goods.

And it was no wonder Allison was failing chem. A ton of her compounds were wrong. She had written down glucose as $C_9H_{12}O_9$ instead of $C_6H_{12}O_6$. Ariana shook her head and started correcting the errors. A cheat sheet would look totally bogus if it was *wrong*.

Suddenly memories of last night rushed upon her unbidden and she blushed from head to toe. Her fingers trembled and she set her pen down, taking a deep breath.

She was not thinking about Palmer now. This morning, in the light of day, her priorities were clear again. She had to get Allison disqualified from the running for Stone and Grave. She had to save her friends, save herself. Whatever she had with Palmer, it wouldn't matter if she was dead.

But this was going to work. It had to. Ariana picked up her pen again and got back to work.

Earlier, when Tahira and Allison had stopped by to grab Kaitlynn and go to breakfast, it had been all Ariana could do to keep from laughing in Allison's haughty face. The girl was going down and she didn't even suspect it. Ariana couldn't wait to see her crumble when her chemistry teacher found the cheat sheet.

She took a deep breath and glanced at the garbage can, in which lay her latest warning from Kaitlynn, hidden underneath a slew of crumpled tissues. Today she'd simply left Ariana a photo of Lexa, Soomie, Maria, and Brigit, printed off one of their Facebook pages, with a sloppy red line slashed across each of their necks. On the bottom was written:

EENIE, MEANIE, MINEY, MO . . . YOU HAVE SIX DAYS! ☺

As far as Ariana knew, no one else had received any ominous gifties. Apparently Kaitlynn had been too drunk last night after her double date to attempt anything more intricate. Thank goodness. If she'd tried, Ariana was sure she would have woken up without a nose or a foot.

There was a quick knock at her door and then it opened. Ariana quickly slid Allison's page under the notebook and turned to a clean one.

"Whatcha doing?" Lexa asked, all smiles. She wore a pair of blue linen shorts, a short-sleeved white blouse with eyelet detailing, and tall espadrilles with thick laces crisscrossing her ankles.

Ariana felt guilty at the very sight of her, knowing that she had betrayed Lexa so very deeply the night before. It didn't matter that Lexa had been out on a date with Conrad, as Ariana had so lamely rationalized last night. She still had feelings for Palmer, and Ariana had made a mockery of those feelings.

She would not do it again. Palmer would simply have to wait until Ariana was sure Lexa was over him.

"Just jotting down some thoughts for the *Ash* meeting on Monday," Ariana replied, turning in her seat. "I want to make sure I'm prepared."

"Oh, April's going to love you," Lexa said with a wave of her hand. She jumped onto Ariana's bed, landing on her knees and bouncing once. "Don't worry about that."

"You're in a good mood," Ariana noted.

Lexa blushed and swung her legs around so that she was sitting on the edge of the bed.

"Well, first of all, there were no pink jewelry boxes lying around this morning, so either the Fellows got bored or they figured out we're on to them," she said. "*And* Conrad and I are spending the whole day together. He's taking me out on his uncle's boat."

"Wow," Ariana said, impressed. "A whole day together. Sounds like you two are going places."

Lexa grinned and toyed with the fringe that was attached to the zipper on her sporty bag. "We may be going to the NoBash together, if today goes well."

Ariana's heart did a series of manic somersaults. This was all so very good. So good that it even eased her guilt, just a bit.

"That's incredible, Lexa. I'm so happy for you," Ariana said.

Lexa got up and put her arms out at her sides. "Palmer who, right?"

"Right." Ariana got up and gave her friend a hug. "Good luck today. I'm sure it's going to be incredible."

"Thanks, Ana," Lexa said with a smile. "And don't think I don't know you had something to do with this."

Ariana's heart skipped a beat. "What do you mean?"

"Inviting Connie to lunch, having him meet up with us everywhere," Lexa said, giving Ariana a sly look. "You're a little matchmaker, aren't you?"

A blush crept up Ariana's neck and onto her cheeks. "You're not mad, are you?"

"Are you kidding? I always knew Connie, but I never really *knew* him," Lexa said. "If it weren't for you, I never would have found out that the perfect guy was jogging past me every morning on the cross-country trail."

"Well then, I'm glad I could help," Ariana replied. "Have fun today."

"I will! See you after dinner!"

Lexa practically spun out of the room, closing the door behind her. When Ariana was sure she was gone, she allowed herself a guilt-free moment of happy dancing in the center of the hardwood floor. Everything was coming together. Today Lexa would ask Conrad to the NoBash, officially freeing up Palmer to be Ariana's date. The girl couldn't expect Palmer to be dateless for the biggest party of the season, especially when she already had someone, right? Tomorrow, Allison would be caught cheating on her chemistry test, and the resulting scandal would get her booted from the running for Stone and Grave. Now all Ariana had to do was secure that NoBash invite for Kaitlynn and all would be right with the world.

Well, that and make a spectacle of herself. But she had an idea—a rather terrifying idea—of how she might be able to accomplish that. She was planning to head into the city later that day to secure the necessary materials. But that was later. For now, she had some handwriting to perfect.

COLLATERAL DAMAGE

The white tile was so cold Ariana could feel it through the fabric of her short-sleeved blue uniform shirt. She shivered slightly but didn't move. She was leaning back against the wall of the bathroom, which was positioned conveniently across the hallway from the classroom in which Allison was currently taking her chemistry exam. If someone walked in, Ariana wanted to appear casually aloof, but she also wanted to keep her position directly across from the door, so that she could be through it the second the tone sounded. Which was also why she had faked stomach cramps to get out of French class early. It pained her to think that her fellow students might think she had IBS or something, but these were necessary sacrifices.

At least Kaitlynn's midnight rampages seemed to be over. Once again, Ariana and her floormates had woken up intact, no random body parts on their bedside tables.

And now Ariana could just focus on the plan. Allison's fake cheat sheet was pinned between Ariana's hip and the outside of her bag. Everything was in place. This was going to work. No one had to die to ensure that Kaitlynn would get into Stone and Grave. A little scandal would suffice.

The tone sounded. Ariana held her bag firmly against her hip and walked out. Tahira was outside the chem room door, obviously waiting for Allison, which gave Ariana a moment's pause. But Tahira's back was to her for the moment, and besides, she couldn't let a tiny hiccup like this stop her. Mr. Chen, the chemistry teacher, opened the door and stood back to let his students out. A few guys rushed out and jogged down the hallway as if they didn't want to miss a moment of free time in the sun. Then Ariana heard Allison's horse laugh, and she took a few steps forward, gaining momentum. The second Allison stepped through the doorway, Ariana took one giant step and slammed into a poor, unsuspecting sophomore girl who was walking in the other direction. The girl pinballed off Ariana and careened into Allison before hitting the floor herself. Allison dropped two notebooks, her chem text, and a pencil on the ground. Ariana shifted her bag and the cheat sheet fluttered down, coming to rest just to the left of the notebooks. Perfection. Then she quickly moved down the hall to watch the action unfold from afar.

"What the hell?" Tahira said, steadying Allison before she could go over as well.

"Are you all right?" the sophomore's friend asked, helping her up.

The girl looked more humiliated than hurt as she scurried to her feet, her dark eyes avoiding everyone else's. Collateral damage. Sometimes it was necessary. "M'fine," she said, scurrying off.

"I'm not," Allison called after the girl, holding on to her arm. "Thanks a lot. That's gonna bruise."

"Do you need to see the nurse, Miss Rothaus?" Mr. Chen asked, pushing his glasses up on his nose with his forefinger.

"No. I'm all right," Allison replied grouchily, rubbing her arm.

Tahira crouched to pick up Allison's stuff. Ariana saw her do a double take when she picked up the cheat sheet. She moved to hide it, but it was too late. Mr. Chen had noticed it too.

"What's this?" Mr. Chen asked, plucking the index card from Tahira's fingers. His glance flitted over the card. Then he fixed Allison with a stern look. "Miss Rothaus?"

Down the hallway, Ariana hid a smile behind her hand. Mr. Chen was playing his part so spot-on she could have written it for him.

"That's not mine," Allison said, her blond curls trembling.

"It certainly looks like your handwriting," Mr. Chen said.

Allison glanced at Tahira, who shrugged an apology. Clearly *she* believed it was Allison's cheat sheet. The small crowd around them grew, sensing impending fodder for gossip.

"I know, but it's not mine," Allison protested. "Honestly, Mr. Chen. I studied my butt off for this test. I didn't need to cheat."

"Nevertheless, the evidence suggests otherwise," Mr. Chen said, fluttering the index card like a taunt. "Come along, Miss Rothaus. I'm afraid we're going to have to have a conversation with the headmaster about this."

Allison's mouth set in a tight white line. "Fine," she said.

Just then Brigit turned the corner and locked eyes with Ariana, giving her a giddy thumbs-up before walking along as if nothing had happened.

Ariana waited while Mr. Chen shut the lights in his classroom and closed the door, then followed him out down the hallway, admirably keeping her head held high. It wasn't until the heavy door slammed behind her that Ariana allowed herself one small, triumphant laugh, which was drowned out by the twittering gossip and speculation that filled the hallway around them.

It was almost too easy.

RETALIATION

"I'm so glad you came to the meeting tonight, Ana," April Corrigan said in her slight Irish accent as she turned out the lights in the multimedia room that evening and ushered Ariana out. "I liked your idea about theming each issue of *The Ash* after the season in which it's published."

"Well, nothing *too* on the nose," Ariana said, tilting her chin. Up ahead, the dozen other members of the literary magazine's staff pushed through the double doors of the building. "I'm thinking maybe coming-of-age for fall, death for winter . . . celebration for spring. Just brainstorming here."

April nodded enthusiastically, checking messages on her iPhone while she adjusted the stack of notebooks and back issues of *The Ash* in her arms.

"We should definitely do it," April said, shoving her square glasses up into her hair to hold her curls back from her face. "Remind me at the next meeting and we can all ruminate on the exact themes together." She fished out a few copies of *The Ash* and handed them to Ariana as they walked out. "In the meantime, why don't you look these over? I'd love to hear your thoughts."

Ariana beamed. April was very accomplished and she had run the meeting like a professional—organized, to the point, succinct but welcoming. Everyone on the staff had hung on her every word. She wasn't going to be wasting anyone's time with a whole lot of flowery debates over whether a piece was worthy for publication or not. Although, as a senior, April was actually two years younger than Ariana, Ariana found herself looking up to the girl as a real junior transfer would have, honored that April was asking for her input.

"That's great. I'll make some notes and bring them next Monday," Ariana replied, tucking the issues into her arms in a neat pile.

"Perfect. Lexa and Soomie were right about you," April said with a smile.

Ariana's heart skipped a beat. "Why? What did they say?"

"Just that you were my kind of girl," April replied, sending a quick text.

Ariana smiled. So maybe the whole "rigid" thing wasn't a curse after all. Maybe it just meant that Ariana was an April kind of girl. And if Lexa and the others were friends with April, then clearly they could accept Ariana the way she was as well.

But she was still going to show them that she wasn't rigid *all* the time.

"Interesting," April said, pausing and pushing her glasses up again.

She looked across the circle, where a bunch of people were jogging past the class building toward the boys' dorms beyond. "Wonder what that's all about."

Ariana and April exchanged an intrigued look and followed the crowd. Standing behind Ferrin Hall, the upperclassman dorm, was a huge crowd of students that was growing larger by the second. A few people pointed up at one of the windows on the top floor and Ariana squinted in the waning light of evening to see what had caught everyone's attention.

Finally, her eyes lit on a window that looked different from the others. As she squinted at it, she realized that something was stuffed up against the windowpane.

"Is that what I think it is?" April asked, narrowing her eyes.

Just then, Landon glanced over his shoulder and spotted Ariana. He whacked Adam on the back of the head to get his attention, and the two boys joined them.

"What's going on?" Ariana asked.

"Some genius filled Martin Tsang's room with coconuts," Landon said, laughing. "Literally filled it! There must be a thousand coconuts in there."

"More, actually," Adam said, twisting his lips in thought. "You'd need at least two thousand to fill a standard ten-by-ten dorm room."

"The genius of it is, Tsang *hates* coconuts," Landon said, still laughing.

"It's true," April confirmed with a nod. "He doesn't just hate them. He's afraid of them."

"How can you be *afraid* of coconuts?" Ariana asked, laughing now as well.

"Who knows? Ask Martin Tsang," Palmer answered, joining them. The sound of his voice sent pleasant shivers all through Ariana's body and into her toes. He slung one arm companionably over Ariana's shoulder, the other over April's. This simple touch brought back a thousand vivid memories of Saturday night, and suddenly Ariana's skin was burning. "Little dude freaked out when he opened the door to his room and all those nasty things came rolling out. He's down at the infirmary talking to Dr. Shrinkhead."

"Dr. Shrinkhead," Ariana repeated, trying to appear unaffected.

"His real name's Dr. Brinkshed, but since he's the campus shrink, the nickname wasn't much of a leap," April explained.

"What I want to know is, how the hell did anyone get that many coconuts onto campus and into his dorm in the middle of the day without anyone noticing?" Palmer said, leaning his weight on Ariana and April now, causing Ariana's body heat to skyrocket. "Whoever did this is a criminal mastermind. In fact, I'd like to meet such a person."

Something in the way he said it made it absolutely clear to Ariana that he was the mastermind in question. She looked at him and smiled.

"I'd like to meet that person too."

Palmer stood up straight and tugged up on the waistband of his pants. "Who knows, Ana," he said, chucking her under the chin with his fist like an uncle might. "Someday, you just might have that chance."

Then he turned and loped away, casually producing his baseball from a back pocket and tossing it up and down as he went. Ariana smiled after him, happy in the knowledge she had just gleaned. As Soomie would put it, the facts were these:

A) This was clearly the retaliation against the Fellows that Lexa had spoken of after the toenail incident, which meant that B) Martin Tsang was in the Fellows, and that C) if Palmer had executed the prank, as Ariana was certain he had, then Palmer was definitely in Stone and Grave.

BACKFIRED

"Looking good!" Ariana said as Brigit teetered by her in her new heels that night. She was sitting in the Wolcott Hall common room with her history books open on the table in front of her, but she hadn't studied much since she'd arrived. She was too busy feeling giddy over the certainty that Palmer was in Stone and Grave. That if she got in—*when* she got in—they would be brought even closer together. And she *was* going to get in, because the Allison plan had clearly worked. No one had seen the girl since Mr. Chen had dragged her off to the headmaster's office that morning. Ariana hoped that meant Allison was in serious trouble. Maybe she'd even been thrown out of APH entirely. A girl couldn't get into Stone and Grave if she wasn't even enrolled at the school.

"I'm glad I *look* good. Because I feel like I'm about to—" Brigit attempted to turn at the far end of the room and tumbled sideways instead, falling over the back of a vacant chair. "Ow."

"Are you all right?" Ariana asked, jumping up.

"Fine. I'm fine. I just have to master this before the NoBash, because it's going to be a lot worse if I do that and the only thing around to break my fall is Ambassador Tate and her wheelchair," Brigit said, her face flushing as she stood up straight.

"Yeah. That would be bad," Ariana agreed.

"Oh, by the way, I gave Lillian an invite," Brigit said, taking a tentative step. "She was so excited she hugged me for like five minutes. I thought she was going to pee in her pants."

Ariana swallowed back all the snide remarks she wanted to make and tried to feel the triumph of successfully completing another task. Kaitlynn was going to the NoBash. Ariana's life was safe. For now.

"That's great. She's a sweet girl," Ariana said with some effort. *When she's not cutting off our hair and nails,* she added silently.

"Yeah. I like her. I'm glad you invited her on Saturday."

A sudden burst of laughter filled the foyer and Ariana turned around slowly. It couldn't be. It just couldn't.

Allison and Tahira traipsed through the door, falling all over each other in giddiness. Ariana felt as if she were being sucked through some kind of wormhole. What was Allison doing here? And why was she so effing happy?

"What's going on?" Ariana asked.

The two girls stopped in their tracks, falling silent. They glanced around the room, which was dotted with students, then exchanged a look.

"I *suppose* we could tell you," Tahira said, though she sounded anything but thrilled at the idea. She glanced over her shoulder at the theater, then waved for Ariana and Brigit to follow them. As soon as the four girls were safely inside the darkened theater, Tahira and Allison started to giggle all over again. "You guys are going to *love* this," Tahira said with a trace of sarcasm.

"You know those tasks we got the other night?" Allison whispered, her eyes twinkling in the dim light coming through the windows from the common room. "Well, I just completed mine."

She and Tahira slapped hands. Ariana's heart plummeted. No. This was not possible. Allison was supposed to be disqualified. She was supposed to be out of the running. And now the girl was telling her that she was one step closer to getting *in*?

"What was it?" Brigit asked.

Allison pulled out her slip of black paper and held it up. "Sabotage a pledge from another secret society," she said with a grin. "You know that cheat sheet Mr. Chen found this morning? Well, it wasn't mine. And as I was sitting in Jansen's office waiting for her and Chen to finish deliberating, all I could think about was who could have done it, and then I realized . . . Justina Cruz—the girl who bumped into me? She was on Team Blue and I *know* she's being tapped because of . . . you know . . . her mom—"

"Her mom?" Ariana interrupted.

Tahira gave Ariana a derisive look. "Yeah. Dora Cruz? Hello? What planet are you from?"

Ariana bit her tongue. Dora Cruz was a famous movie star, and apparently the fact that this Justina girl was her daughter was common knowledge at APH. To everyone other than Ariana.

"*Anyway*, I told Jansen and Chen that it must have been her. That she was setting me up," Allison continued.

"And they believed you?" Ariana asked.

"They took a second look at the cheat sheet and found some differences between it and Allison's handwriting," Tahira said. "She has this weird dyslexic thing where her sixes are nines and her nines are sixes—"

"And Mr. Chen always gives me a pass on it because he knows I can't control it," Allison interrupted. "So when he saw that all the compounds on the cheat sheet were correct, he figured it out right away."

Tahira looked Ariana directly in the eye. "It was an *obvious* fake."

Ariana wanted to scream. She'd fixed all those compounds because she thought the girl was an idiot, not a mild dyslexic. This could not be happening. How could her plan to get rid of Allison have worked out in Allison's *favor*? The room started to spin. This was wrong. This was so very, very wrong.

"Maybe *her* task was to sabotage *me*!" Allison said. "Who knows? Whatever the case, they gave her a month's detention and there's no way she's getting in to whatever society wanted her. And ta-da! My task is done!"

She threw her arms over her head and danced in a circle, all proud of herself. Ariana's fingertips twitched, itching to shove her over the back row of seats. Her throat started to close over and her vision began to blur. Allison had completed her task. There were still five of them vying for four open spots. And once again, Ariana's life was at stake. All their lives. Her stomach filled with acidic dread. All that work had come to nothing. *Nothing.* And suddenly, Ariana couldn't breathe.

No. You cannot let them see how this is affecting you. Control, Ariana. Control.

In, one . . . two . . . three . . .

Out, one . . . two . . . three . . .

In, one . . . two . . . three . . .

Out, one . . . two . . . three . . .

"Come on, Allison. Let's go pop open that Taittinger Daddy sent," Tahira said, tugging on her friend's elbow. "We need to celebrate. See you later, ladies!"

She and Allison slipped out, leaving Ariana and Brigit alone. The moment they were gone, Ariana sucked in her first good breath in a long while. She leaned both hands on the back of a theater seat and took another.

"Well. That backfired," Brigit said.

"What backfired?"

Ariana's hand flew to her throat, startled. Lexa was standing in the doorway of the theater, holding it open.

"You scared me," she said.

"Sorry," Lexa replied. "So what backfired?"

"We played a prank on Allison this morning," Brigit replied, leaning back against the rear row of seats and kicking off her heels. She sighed happily as the stilettos hit the floor. "But it looks like she took the lemons and turned them into a lemon-tini."

"Wait a minute, that was you guys?" Lexa said, letting the door close behind her. She crossed her slim arms over her chest. "You're the ones who set up the fake cheat sheet?"

"It was Ana's idea," Brigit said helpfully. "We thought we'd have a little fun with her. You know, since she was such a beyotch to Ana when they were living together."

"You're kidding," Lexa said flatly, giving Ariana a scolding look.

"What's the big deal?" Ariana asked. "We were just messing around."

She had thought that, of all people, Lexa would be pleased. She was the one who was apparently so obsessed with getting "Briana Leigh" to loosen up and be like her old self. The one who most likely had decided that Ariana's task should be to make a "spectacle" of herself.

"Just messing around? This is serious stuff! She could have gotten thrown out of school." Lexa's eyes narrowed.

Ariana's face burned. Had she been right all along? Was it a bad thing to try to sabotage another potential member of Stone and Grave? But no. It wasn't possible—Soomie and Maria had practically *told* her to do it. Unless they were trying to sabotage *her*. Did they actually want to keep her out? That couldn't be. They were her friends.

Suddenly, Ariana's head hurt from trying to figure out what it all meant, what everyone's motivations were. But one thing was for certain: Lexa did not get to be her moral center. The girl had *no* idea the sacrifices Ariana was currently making to preserve their friendship *and* spare her feelings. And to keep everyone on this campus safe.

"She would have ended up at some other good school," Ariana said, lifting a hand. "It's not that big a deal."

Lexa sighed and shook her head. "Whatever. I'm *glad* it backfired," she said. "You two totally stepped over the line." She turned around and flung open the door. "I'll see you upstairs."

As the door closed behind her, Brigit gave Ariana a chagrined look. "Wow. She was pissed."

"I don't get it," Ariana said. "I thought she *wanted* me to loosen up."

Brigit shrugged. "I guess in Lexa's world there's loosening up in a good way and loosening up in a bad way."

Ariana gripped her forearm tightly in her fingers. She couldn't believe Lexa was mad at her. All she was trying to do was protect her. Protect Brigit, Maria, Soomie, Tahira, and Allison too. There was a psychopath out there just waiting to prey on one of them, and Ariana was the only person who could stop her. Every single fiber of her being was focused on trying to stop her.

But she had failed. And now there was no telling what Kaitlynn might do. Whom she might hurt. Because of Ariana's mistakes, someone—most likely someone she cared about—was going to die.

"Ana?" Brigit said, looking worriedly at Ariana's arm. "Are you okay?"

Ariana released her grip. There were four perfectly straight white lines where her fingers had been. The rest of her arm was red from the pressure.

"I have to go," she said, whipping the door open. "I have to get out of here."

It wasn't until she was out in the open air and halfway down the hill that she let the tears flow.

FAILURES

Ariana was aware of a sharp pain in her leg before she was even aware that she was awake. She swatted at it as she lifted her head and opened her groggy eyes. Her hand hit something hard and she sat up straight. Her heart stopped. She was looking right into the menacing eyes of Kaitlynn Nottingham, and Kaitlynn was holding a steak knife. Red liquid dripped from the tip.

Ariana gasped. A puddle of blood had pooled on her sheet, flowing from a small gash across her shin. Suddenly, she was wide awake. She jumped to her feet, knocking Kaitlynn backward with all her might, gritting her teeth to keep from screaming out in rage and pain. Kaitlynn reared backward and tried to grab a desk chair for balance but crashed to the floor on her ass anyway. The knife skittered across the hardwood and came to rest under Ariana's bed.

"What the hell are you doing?" Ariana whisper-shouted. She stood over Kaitlynn, her cut stinging, unable to take even a second to check

the severity of the wound. She couldn't turn her back on Kaitlynn. Couldn't let her defenses down for even a second. The psycho had finally crossed a line.

Kaitlynn scrambled to her feet and got right in Ariana's face. "That's your brilliant plan? Get Allison caught *cheating*? What do you think this is, some kind of Disney Channel special?"

"I was *trying* to get the job done without anyone getting hurt," Ariana replied through her teeth. "See, Kaitlynn, when people get hurt or *murdered* it kind of draws attention to the situation. And that's the last thing either of us wants."

"You're an idiot," Kaitlynn said, pacing over to her bed. "All you've done is wasted your time and mine. Now I have to figure out a way to off the competition and I only have a few days to do it."

Ariana wanted to scream. She wanted to scream so badly she felt as if her throat, her brain, and her heart were all going to explode.

"Didn't you hear a word I just said?" she hissed. "We cannot have a murder on campus, Kaitlynn. If anyone dies, we all get interviewed. And if you and I get interviewed, they are going to realize the truth about us."

Kaitlynn looked off toward the door. "It's just going to be so hard deciding who has to go," she said, as if she were talking about figuring out which coat to wear. "Although technically, it should be you," she added, gesturing at Ariana. "You're obviously a waste of space."

Groaning in desperation, Ariana grabbed the nearest thing she could find to stanch the bleeding on her leg, which just happened to be Kaitlynn's white APH hoodie. She held it over her cut and winced against the pain. Sitting down on her own bed, she held her breath and counted to ten.

"You said I had until Saturday night, remember?" Ariana spoke slowly.

Kaitlynn glanced up. "Yeah. So?"

"So, be patient. I'll take care of it. I still have five days," Ariana said. She carefully removed the sweatshirt. It stuck to the wound for a moment, then peeled away, leaving a trail of sharp pain. Ariana gritted her teeth as she looked over the wound. It was ugly but not too deep. It didn't look as if she would need stitches.

"You'll take care of it," Kaitlynn said dubiously.

"Yes. I said I would, and I will," Ariana replied, though she had absolutely no idea how. All she knew was that she had to protect her friends and herself, whatever the cost.

"Fine. If you say so," Kaitlynn said with a shrug. Then she lay back on her bed and pulled the covers over her, as if nothing more had happened than a quick midnight chat between friends. "Good night, Ariana. Oh, and you owe me a sweatshirt."

Then she turned on her side, her back facing Ariana, and promptly fell asleep.

For a long few minutes, Ariana sat there, listening to Kaitlynn breathe, marveling over the depths of the girl's psychosis, holding the sweatshirt to her leg. Then, ever so carefully, she crouched to her knees, leaned down, and extracted the bloody steak knife from under her bed. It was one of the knives they used at the dining hall. Ariana wondered when Kaitlynn had stolen it, and whether there were any more like it hidden in their room.

Slowly, she stood up, gripping the handle of the knife in her sweaty, blood-caked palm. She imagined herself driving the blade into Kaitlynn's back. The look of confusion and pain and reproach in Kaitlynn's terrified eyes.

Ariana breathed in and out, matching the cadence of her breath to Kaitlynn's, clutching the knife—her salvation—in her grip. And then, finally, the moment passed. She knew she couldn't do it, even though it would be so very satisfying. So very justified. If she murdered Kaitlynn in their shared dorm room, she would be back at the Brenda T. by tomorrow night. It couldn't be. And that frustrated her more than any of the failures she had endured over the last few days.

Sooner or later, Kaitlynn would get hers. The universe had a way of working these things out. Ariana simply hoped she would be there when justice was served. That she would have some part, even the smallest part, in making it happen.

THE BULLDOZER

Tuesday afternoon after classes, Ariana was walking across campus toward the tennis courts when she spotted Palmer coming out of the library. Her breath caught in her throat at the mere sight of him. Her first instinct was to avoid him. Lexa hadn't asked Conrad to the NoBash yet, so the two were not officially together. But Ariana had suffered a rough night. She deserved a bit of a flirt. Besides, Lexa's holier-than-thou act had seriously pissed her off.

He spotted her before she reached him and his eyes traveled up and down her practice uniform appreciatively, taking in the navy blue APH polo and white miniskirt. But then, of course, he frowned at the large bandage around her leg.

"Hey," he said, pausing in front of her. He took a quick look around, and, finding the coast apparently clear, lifted her hand to kiss it. "What happened to your leg?"

"Midnight snack accident," Ariana replied, lifting a shoulder. "Never take the stairs when half-asleep."

"Sound advice," Palmer said, removing his baseball from his bag and tossing it up in front of him. "Can I walk you to practice?"

"Sure," Ariana replied with a smile.

As they strolled south toward the playing fields on the outskirts of campus, Ariana took a deep, soothing breath and let it out. Autumn was finally coming. She could taste it in the air. It was the first crisp, clear day of the season and the leaves on the trees of the APH campus were finally beginning to turn. She was walking along a cobblestone path with the guy of her dreams. For the briefest of moments, she allowed herself a break. Allowed herself to enjoy what she had—to appreciate how far she'd come.

"So, how's everything going?" Palmer asked. "I hear you went to the *Ash* meeting on Monday. April Corrigan thinks you're going to be her new star editor."

"Really?" Ariana said, her cheeks flushing pink. "That was nice of her to say."

"So things are good?" Palmer asked.

"I suppose," Ariana said, adjusting the thick strap on her white Lacoste tennis bag. Her first week of classes had gone well, but keeping up with her work was about the only thing she had achieved on her long list of goals.

"That's convincing," Palmer said sarcastically, tossing the ball up and catching it. "I hope . . . You're not regretting the other night, are you?"

Ariana's toes curled at the mere thought of "the other night." "No," she said. "I'm not. I promise."

"Good." Palmer looked genuinely relieved. "Because I've kind of been waiting for you to show up at my door again," he whispered, his voice low and sexy.

Ariana smiled. "I will. I mean . . . eventually. I just . . . There's been a lot going on."

Palmer paused and looked down at her, his face creased with concern. "Is everything okay?"

Ariana thought of Stone and Grave, and how Allison had closed one of the spots. She thought of Kaitlynn wielding her bloody knife in the middle of the night. Thought of how Lexa and Conrad were taking it so slow they were practically glacial. Thought of that stupid slip of black paper and the task upon it, which she had yet to get up the guts to complete. When it came to life at APH, she wasn't exactly overachieving.

"I guess I just didn't expect everything to be so hard," she summed up finally, pausing at a bend in the path.

"Ah." Palmer paused as well. He turned to face her, dropped the ball back into his bag, and crossed his arms over his chest. "Ana Covington, you are about to get one of Palmer Liriano's patented pep talks."

Ariana smiled. "Am I? Lucky me."

"You're lucky. I don't just give these out to anyone," he said. Then he reached up and tucked an errant hair behind her ear. A pleasant shiver shot down her side. "But for you, anything."

Ariana beamed.

"The first day I met you, Ana, I knew you could do anything," Palmer said. "You just have that look about you. Like nothing's ever going to stand in your way. So whatever speed bumps you think you've hit since you've been here, just drive over them. *Bulldoze* over them. Because I know you can."

"Wow," Ariana breathed, her heart full. "That was one sucky metaphor, Palmer Liriano."

He laughed. "All right. You got me. My pep talks suck. How's this." He took her hand, lifted it so that her palm was facing his, and laced his fingers through hers. "Will you go to the NoBash with me?"

Ariana bit her lip, her mind flitting over Lexa. Over Lexa and Palmer together at the beginning of the year. Over Lexa's tears in the bathroom and then again in her dorm room. And then the images were gone. And once they were gone, she was left staring at her own hand entwined with Palmer's. And suddenly, she didn't care about anything else.

"Yes," she said firmly.

Palmer's eyes widened in surprise. "Yes?"

"Yes," Ariana said with a nod. Then Tahira came around the corner and Ariana instinctively dropped Palmer's hand. A look of confusion crossed his face. "But let's keep it quiet. Just for now," she said, glancing at Tahira.

She couldn't let anyone know she was with Palmer until Lexa made it official with Conrad. People would think she'd moved in too fast.

Palmer's jaw set, and for a moment Ariana was afraid he was going to rescind the invite, but he simply nodded. "Okay. If that's the way you want it. I'll see you later, Ana."

"'Bye," Ariana said, feeling a whoosh of loss as he turned to go.

He greeted Tahira as he walked by her and strolled off, plucking his baseball out of his bag again.

"Hello Ana," Tahira said, stopping in front of her.

Her thick hair was up in a high ponytail, and gaudy gold earrings dangled from her ears. She was wearing the exact same practice uniform as Ariana, but several of the buttons on her polo were undone. The girl just couldn't handle the idea of modesty, even while working out.

"What do you want?" Ariana asked.

"Touchy, touchy," Tahira said, twirling the handle of her aluminum racket with one hand. "Have I done something to upset you?"

"Not today," Ariana replied coolly. She started to walk toward the courts again and Tahira fell into step at her side. There were already several people warming up, lobbing balls across the nets, and Ariana felt a thrill of anticipation rush through her. After her encounter with Palmer, she was very much in the mood to kick a little tennis ass.

He thought she could do anything. Bulldoze over anyone. Actually, now that she thought about it, she kind of liked that metaphor.

"I think you mean, 'Not *yet*,'" Tahira corrected. She placed her fingers firmly on Ariana's arm, stopping her.

Ariana narrowed her eyes at Tahira. Where, exactly, was this going?

"I know it was you who set up Allison," Tahira said.

Ariana didn't move, didn't blink, didn't breathe. She didn't betray one hint of nervousness over the fact that she'd just been very, very snagged.

"Oh, really?" she said.

Tahira laughed. "Like it was just some coincidence that you happened to be in that hallway? I saw you bump into Justina and practically shove her into Allison. You're not as stealthy as you think you are."

Ariana's jaw clenched.

"Besides, I know Justina Cruz," Tahira said, twirling her racket again. "She doesn't have the balls to go up against me and Allison, even if it is for membership in Scarlet Key."

A sizzle of intrigue shot through Ariana. The third society was named Scarlet Key?

"You have no proof," Ariana replied finally, clutching the strap on her tennis bag.

Tahira laughed. "I don't need proof. I don't intend to turn you in. Not for *this*, anyway."

Something in her tone made Ariana's blood turn to icy slush.

"What does *that* mean?"

Tahira took a step toward her, so close her breasts grazed Ariana's arm. Ariana flinched at the intimate contact but didn't back away. She couldn't let Tahira see her sweat.

"Here's the deal, *Ana*," Tahira said. "Stay away from me, stay away from my friends, and I might consider not telling the administration who was responsible for all those thefts at the beginning of the year."

Ariana took an instinctive step back. She couldn't help it. But the moment she did, she realized her mistake. Her action made her look as guilty as she was. And Tahira slowly smiled.

"How did you—"

"Let's just say a little bird told me," Tahira said snootily. "It would be so fun to bring you down. Problem is, we're both up for membership in Stone and Grave, and they kind of frown upon things like turning on a potential sister or brother."

Ariana blinked.

"I guess you didn't know that, since you've already done it," Tahira said, clearly enjoying every ounce of misery she was spreading on so thick. "Still, *I* would be justified turning you in, A, if I really wanted to."

There was no air. Gray spots started to form before Ariana's eyes, obscuring her view of Tahira. Suddenly, Ariana was grateful for the cool breeze skittering over her hot-as-tar skin.

"See, my task is to humiliate a donor," Tahira continued. "And I just happen to know that you and your grandma donated a ton of cash to get your ass into this place, so you qualify. If I have to, I'm going to see that it's you who gets humiliated. And probably arrested. So like I said, back off."

Ariana tried to think of something to say. Something that would save even the tiniest bit of dignity, but her mind was a complete, panicked, blank.

"Good," Tahira said with a smirk. "I'm glad we had this little chat."

Then she turned and flounced away, her tennis skirt swishing with every step. Ariana slowly backed onto a stone bench that was positioned off to the side of the walkway and sat down, her mind racing. Who had told Tahira? Who else knew what she had done other than—

Kaitlynn. Of course. She must have told Tahira just to amuse her. Just to win her over. And now Tahira was going to use the information to hold Ariana under her manicured thumb.

But not for long.

Just like that, everything snapped back into focus. Tahira hadn't completed her task yet. Her spot was still open.

THE SPECTACLE

Ariana walked into the dining hall on Wednesday morning, her shoulders back, her jaw set in grim determination. Huge, white-framed sunglasses covered her eyes and she wore a hot pink feather boa around her neck, over her uniform. In one hand she gripped the leather handle of a small but powerful speaker. In the other were her iPod and a microphone.

Now that she had decided to do away with Tahira, it was time to ensure her own spot in Stone and Grave—time to get this spectacle thing over with. Time to show Lexa and Palmer and Soomie and Maria and whoever the hell else was in Stone and Grave just how serious she was about getting in.

She caught a few curious looks and snickers of interest as she wove her way to her usual table, smack-dab in the center of the action. Soomie and Maria were already seated, Soomie reading a book, Maria texting on her phone, but everyone else was loitering around, getting the morning gossip. As soon as Ariana dropped the speaker on the table with a clang and climbed atop the wooden surface next to it, however, conversation quieted considerably.

Ariana looked down at the two girls, wondering if they had known she was going to sabotage Allison and if they had been sabotaging her by encouraging it. Or had they simply assumed Ariana was too smart to get caught? She wasn't sure, but either way, now was not the time to try to figure it out. She had a task to complete.

"Um, Ana?" Soomie said, placing her book aside and sitting forward. "What the hell are you doing?"

"This," Ariana replied.

She bent down, attached the iPod and mic to the speaker, and flipped on the power. Her heart was pounding harder than it had in a long time. Definitely since the night she'd made her harrowing escape from the Brenda T. But at least then she'd had a plan. At least then she'd known what she was doing. Right now, she was flying by the seat of her lacy La Perlas.

"Good morning, Atherton-Pryce Hall!" Ariana shouted into the microphone.

An earsplitting peal of feedback sent everyone in a ten-table radius wincing, but it had the desired effect. Every student and teacher in the dining hall, every waiter and custodian, stopped and stared. Lexa, who was standing near the far wall with April, Brigit, and Conrad, took a few steps forward, her jaw dropped in confusion. Oddly, no one made a move to stop her.

"My name is Ana Covington and this is my favorite song," Ariana continued, holding the microphone a bit farther away from her mouth to avoid the feedback issue. Her palm was so slick with sweat she was certain the mic was going to fall from her hand at any second and bounce onto the floor. She hit the play button on the iPod and the opening, electronic notes of Metro Station's "Shake It" blasted through the speaker.

At her feet, Maria and Soomie exchanged a dumbfounded glance. Ariana took a deep breath . . . and started to dance.

That was when the laughter rose up in earnest.

You can do this, Ariana. You can, you can, you can.

Soomie covered her mouth with both hands. Maria laughed and shook her head, looking down at her lap. All across the cafeteria, people were either pointing and laughing or shooting her looks of obvious pity. Ariana tuned it all out and concentrated on the end that would definitely justify these means.

Stone and Grave. This ridiculous spectacle was going to get her into Stone and Grave.

And then Ariana started to sing.

"'I'll take you home if you don't leave me by the front door. . . .'"

"Whoo! Go Ana!" Brigit shouted, raising her hands above her head.

Ariana smiled her thanks, but at this point her eyes were so blurred over by tense tears and sweat, she couldn't entirely make her out in the crowd.

"'Your body's cold, but boy we're getting so warm. . . .'"

This elicited cheers and hollers from the guys nearest to her table.

Students started to crowd forward from every corner of the room, wanting to get to the table first, wanting to see this outrageous display up close. Ariana could hardly stand the attention, all the eyes on her, the expectant grins and the cheers, but she kept on working it. Kept singing and dancing, doing a little twist, taking it down toward the table and back up again. Every new move inspired more cheers, and soon the student body was clapping to the beat. By the time Ariana reached the chorus, they were singing along.

"'Shake shake! Shake shake shake it!'"

The table gyrated under Ariana's feet. She took a second to steady herself and realized with some gratification that it was the result of dozens of people jumping up and down in support. Her heart was still slamming painfully, but her body heat began to normalize and her vision cleared. That was when she spotted Palmer and couldn't help laughing. He was holding up his cell phone like a lighter at the back of the crowd, waving it slowly back and forth with a faux-dazed look of admiration on his face.

After that, Ariana really let loose.

And in less than three minutes it was over. The dining hall erupted in appreciative applause. Ariana took a quick bow and jumped down from the table. She looked at her friends. Maria held up a torn sheet of notebook paper on which she'd hastily scribbled a 10. Soomie held up a 9.5.

"Thank you, thank you," Ariana said.

"What the heck was that all about?" Lexa asked, grabbing her hand.

As if she didn't know.

"The other day Brigit reminded me of those duets we used to do at camp and I guess I just felt inspired," Ariana replied, playing the game.

"Well, then you should have asked me to sing with you," Lexa said. "I definitely would have backed you up."

"Thanks," Ariana replied, dropping into a chair next to her speaker. "But this was meant to be a solo."

Brigit gave Ariana a hug from behind and whispered in her ear. "Nice job, Ana. That was a spectacle if I ever saw one."

Ariana beamed. She didn't even care that she was probably going to be talked about for the rest of the day. Maybe even weeks. Maybe even years. It would all be worth it.

As the waiter appeared to take their orders and the students settled in at their own tables, Ariana felt perfectly at ease. Still breathless, but at ease. She'd done it.

Lexa and Conrad sat down across from her and Ariana blinked. They were holding hands. Lexa saw Ariana notice, and grinned.

"Does this mean . . . ?" Ariana said.

Rather than answer, Lexa leaned forward so she could see Brigit. "Hey Bridge, Conrad's going to be my plus-one for the NoBash. In case you need to notify the calligrapher."

"Really?" Brigit squealed, clapping her hands. "I'm texting her right now!"

"That's so great, you guys," Ariana said.

"I think so," Conrad said, leaning back and putting his arm around

Lexa. "Although I *am* just using her for the invite. I've been hearing about this party for years."

"Shut up," Lexa said, whacking his chest with the back of her hand. Lexa smiled surreptitiously at Ariana as the waiter worked his way around the table to Connie. "Thank you," she mouthed.

"You're welcome," Ariana whispered back. She glanced across the crowded dining hall at the crew table, where Palmer had been taking most of his meals. He wasn't looking her way, but she smiled nonetheless. A huge obstacle had just been cleared for them—bulldozed, perhaps—and he didn't even know it yet.

"Nice singing, Ana," Kaitlynn said as she glided past their table. "I didn't know you had it in you." Then she leaned down next to Ariana's ear and whispered so that only she could hear. "Looks like you've just solidified your spot in Stone and Grave. Too bad that means someone else is going to have to go."

"Not to worry, *Lil*," Ariana said facetiously. "By the time the NoBash is over, we'll both have what we want."

Kaitlynn stood up, shot Ariana an intrigued glance, then gave the table a perfectly sweet and innocent smile and walked away.

"What was that all about?" Lexa asked.

"Oh, just some roommate business," Ariana replied, reaching for her water glass. "Now, what do you guys want to hear for my encore?"

Everyone laughed and started throwing out names of ridiculous songs. Ariana relaxed into her chair and breathed easy for the first time in days. Finally, *finally* things were looking up.

ARM CANDY

Dressed in her strapless, crushed silk gown, her auburn hair pinned back from her face, Ariana felt more beautiful than she had since becoming Briana Leigh. More like herself. For the first time in days, she had everything under control. For the first time in days, she knew exactly how her night was going to end. And it wasn't going to be under Kaitlynn's knife or her scissors or her nail clipper. By the end of the night, Kaitlynn would be satisfied. Her membership in Stone and Grave would be a lock—as long as she completed her own task, which was not Ariana's responsibility—and everyone would be happy.

Except, of course, Tahira and her friends and family. But that was not Ariana's concern.

"This is going to be the greatest NoBash ever!" Brigit announced, raising her video camera in the air to take in the scene outside Wolcott Hall. The two dozen glammed-up students milling around out front cheered in response, hamming it up for the camera. Ariana, standing with Soomie, Maria, Landon, and Christian—all of whom had received their own invites and were therefore going "stag"—waved and laughed as the camera lens passed by her.

"Where's your roommate?" Soomie asked, adjusting her black velvet wrap, which rested in the crook of her arms. She wore a tasteful, gunmetal strapless gown and a simple diamond necklace, her hair pulled back in a tight bun. Pretty, but she could have been Noelle Lange's tightly wound mother headed for the opera.

"Who knows?" Ariana said airily.

And who cares? she added silently.

The last time she had seen Kaitlynn, she had been cursing at her mascara wand in the bathroom. It would be the icing on the cake of her week if Kaitlynn somehow managed to miss the limo caravan to the party. Ariana barely dared to dream. She glanced around the crowd for Palmer, who had never shown up at the door of her room as she assumed he would. Perhaps he had expected to meet her here with everyone else. Although she would have preferred the formality of being picked up at her room, she was too giddy at the thought of being with him to care all that much. She couldn't wait to see what he thought of her gown.

Then, as if thought alone had conjured them out of thin air, Ariana spotted Kaitlynn near the curb, once again blatantly flirting with Palmer. Palmer wore his black tuxedo like the style was made exclusively for him. Ariana hadn't seen anyone look so comfortable in a suit since Thomas Pearson first semi-seduced her at the Winter Ball all those years ago. As Kaitlynn's fingertips fell lightly on Palmer's arm,

Ariana felt a surge of proprietary ire she also hadn't felt in years. Not since the day she'd first seen Thomas talking to Reed Brennan on the Easton Academy quad. The day she'd lost him forever.

That was not going to happen again.

"Excuse me for a moment, ladies," Ariana said, squaring her shoulders.

She strode over to Palmer and slipped up next to him, nudging his arm with her elbow.

"Hey," she said with a just-for-him smile.

He looked down at her. "Hey," he said flatly.

Ariana's heart skipped a beat as trepidation zipped over her skin.

"Hello, Ana. You look . . . cute," Kaitlynn said snootily.

And you look like a skank, Ariana thought, checking out Kaitlynn's ridiculous cleavage in her red, sweetheart-neckline dress.

"Lillian," Ariana replied, looking down her nose at her roommate. "Mind if I talk to Palmer for a sec? Alone?"

Kaitlynn glanced at Palmer, as if expecting him to tell Ariana off. Instead he took a breath and blew it out noisily. "Actually, I do need to speak to Ana, Lillian. If you don't mind."

Ariana's heart did a victory dance as Kaitlynn's face fell ever so slightly. "No problem," she said to Palmer. "I'll catch up with you later."

Then she floated off to join Tahira and Rob in the crowd. Palmer stared out across the driveway toward the valley below, purposely avoiding Ariana's gaze. Her nerves sizzled as she wondered what was wrong. Had Kaitlynn said something bad about her?

"So . . . are you my date for this thing or what?" Ariana said lightly.

"I don't know. You tell me," Palmer said, turning to her. He didn't appear angry, just hurt. Ariana felt a surge of confusion. She was capable of hurting Palmer Liriano?

"What do you mean?" Ariana asked.

"I mean, the last time I talked to you about it, you still didn't want to tell anyone, even though Lexa's been parading all over campus with her tongue down Conrad Royce's throat," Palmer said, color starting to rise from his neck to his face. Ariana felt the sting of this comment. He was hurt, but not entirely by her. He was hurt by Lexa's ability to move on so quickly. And probably by the fact that Ariana had not allowed him to do the same, by keeping him at arm's length. "So you tell me. Am I your date or not?"

Ariana was opening her mouth to respond, when a slim arm looped around hers.

"Is this guy bothering you?" Lexa joked.

She looked drop-dead gorgeous in an emerald green gown that brought out the color of her eyes. It was cut low in the front, even lower in back, and had a multilayered skirt that accentuated the curve of her hips before cascading to the ground. Conrad was right on her heels, looking square and strong in his tuxedo.

Palmer looked into Ariana's eyes. Ariana searched for the perfect thing to say. A way to make it seem as if the fact that Palmer was her date was no big deal—to telegraph to Lexa that it meant nothing—while solidifying to Palmer that it meant everything.

"Come on, Ana," Lexa said, tugging her away. "Christian's dateless too, so I promised him you would be his arm candy. You don't mind if I steal her away, do you, Palmer?"

Palmer's eyes never left Ariana's. He was waiting for her to speak. Waiting for her to tell the truth. But the words were caught in Ariana's throat. Clearly Lexa wanted to get her away from Palmer. Clearly she still didn't want anyone near him. And as long as Ariana was certain Lexa could blackball her from Stone and Grave, she had to keep the girl happy. Palmer could blackball her too, of course, but she believed he was more of a gentleman than that. She believed he would understand that her motives here were pure. And she hoped that he believed, as she did, that all this waiting was just temporary.

"No," Palmer said finally, as if he could follow the train of Ariana's thoughts in her eyes. "I don't mind at all."

Even though it had been Ariana's decision, she felt as if he'd just driven a knife through her heart. But she allowed Lexa to pull her away from Palmer and toward Christian. As she went, she glanced back at Palmer, hoping to convey an apology with her eyes, and saw Kaitlynn already swooping in on him again.

A white-hot bolt of rage shot through Ariana so fiercely, she thought for a moment that she wouldn't be able to contain it. Screw Lexa for snatching her away from Palmer. Lexa already had a new beau. She didn't need the old one. And screw Kaitlynn for homing in on the one guy Ariana wanted. There were plenty of hot, wealthy guys at this school. Couldn't she let Ariana have *anything* for herself?

As she tore her gaze away from Palmer and his leech, Ariana saw that she and Lexa were passing right by Tahira, Allison, and Rob. Her heart skipped a panicked beat at having nearly missed such a perfect opportunity. She reached into her bag, extracted the key from her safety-deposit box—she wouldn't be needing it anymore. She fingered the heavy metal keychain she'd attached to it, then slid it into the outside pocket on Tahira's gold, jewel-encrusted clutch, which was lying on a bench with Allison's bag and their wraps. Instantly, Ariana's body heat cooled.

No one had seen. Step one of her plan was complete.

"Christian, your arm candy as promised," Lexa said, practically flinging Ariana at Christian.

"Nice," Christian said, looking Ariana up and down. "I'll try not to devour you all in one bite."

Landon, Maria, Conrad, Lexa, and Soomie all laughed, while Brigit and Adam had the innocence to blush. Ariana, for her part, simply glanced at her watch and checked the drive for the still elusive limos.

Suddenly she couldn't wait for this night to be over.

PHASE TWO

Ariana stared out the window of the black stretch limousine as it whipped past the long, snaking line of luxury cars waiting to be cleared by the Norwegian embassy's security team. Curious partygoers strained their necks to get a glimpse of the car with the Norwegian flags adorning its front grill, wondering which of Norway's esteemed dignitaries were inside.

Imagine what they would have thought if they could have seen inside and spotted Landon Jacobs downing a thick, dark Guinness from a can while Palmer and Christian cheered him on and Brigit, the beloved princess of Norway, curled into a corner screeching and laughing, just hoping he wouldn't spit it all out all over her.

"Ah. That's the stuff," Landon said, lifting the larger-than-usual-size beer can over his head. "Thanks to the good people of Ireland for that."

Then he belched. Long and loud. Even Soomie looked disgusted.

"Ah, the things you've learned on your world travels," Maria intoned jokingly.

"Yeah, maybe on next year's tour you could, I don't know, take in a museum or two," Lexa joked.

"If they'll pay me to sing, I'm in," Landon replied.

"You're such a fame whore," Maria said, crossing her arms over her chest.

"Ah, but that's why you love me," Landon replied, jostling her with his elbow.

Maria blushed and got up to sit next to Lexa, clearly not wanting anyone in the car to take that love comment seriously. Lexa, meanwhile, looked plenty in love herself. She cuddled into the crook of Conrad's arm and he leaned in to kiss her forehead. Lexa smiled, then glanced out of the corner of her eye to make sure Palmer was watching. He wasn't. He was looking, instead, at Ariana. Quickly, Ariana trained her gaze out the window again as the limo turned onto the circular brick drive leading up to the embassy. Pretending to be oblivious to both Palmer and Lexa was key at this point. The last thing she wanted to do tonight was answer a bunch of Lexa's questions about why Palmer kept staring at her. The go-to answer would be *I have no idea what you're talking about.* But she wasn't sure how long she could keep that up.

"We're here!" Brigit announced merrily as the car came to a stop.

Outside, a hundred camera lenses flanking the red carpet turned to face them. Ariana could hear the helicopters circling overhead, and saw at least a half-dozen uniformed guards stationed along the front lines of the crowd. A red carpet led up to the front door of the mansion that was the embassy, and the whole façade glittered with light.

"I have to go last, you guys. You know the drill," Brigit said. Adam clutched her hand, looking pale and clammy. Apparently the reality of exactly whom he was dating had just hit home full force.

"I'm on it," Landon said.

He flung open the door of the limousine and stepped out, his arms raised above his head. Instantly there was a communal gasp, followed by a cheer.

"Oh my God! Is that Landon Jacobs?" someone shouted. And suddenly, flashbulbs shattered the night, clicking and blinking and winking like a thousand psychotic fireflies. Landon strolled down the red carpet solo, posing here, chatting with a reporter there. The guy knew exactly how to work a crowd.

"At least he's good for creating a diversion," Maria said under her breath, holding the skirt of her dark pink gown as she stepped out.

"Come on. He's good for *way* more than that," Soomie said, following after her with starry eyes.

Christian jumped out and reached back for Ariana's hand. "Milady."

Ariana shot him a smile, but got out on her own. "Sorry, Chris, but I'm not anyone's arm candy," she said, patting him on the arm. "Save me a dance, though."

Christian's face fell, but he recovered quickly, sidling up next to Maria. Random Boy's feelings were the last thing on Ariana's mind. After her tiff with Palmer, this night had become all about work. She glanced over her shoulder at the next limo, which had transported Kaitlynn,

Tahira, and Zuri, plus Allison—whom Brigit had invited because she was a Stone and Grave potential—among others. Ariana had to wait for them to get out of the car without making it too obvious.

"I'd never call you arm candy," Palmer whispered to her as he slipped by. Then he slapped Christian on the back and the two of them walked into the party together.

Lexa and Conrad were next out of the car. Lexa put on a big grin for the paparazzi and Ariana heard a few whispers of "Lexa Greene" and "senator's daughter" skitter through the crowd. She looped her arm through Conrad's and looked at Ariana.

"You coming, Ana?"

"Actually, I'm going to wait for Lily," Ariana replied, her smile forced. "I'll be right in."

"Okay."

Lexa and Conrad walked the red carpet, looking every bit the movie-star couple. Ariana wished Lexa would fully invest herself in the guy already. She seemed to really like him, so why did it also seem like part of her simply wanted to make Palmer jealous?

Kaitlynn, Allison, and Zuri were piling out of the rear car now. Allison and Zuri made their way up the red carpet, arms linked, posing for the cameras as Kaitlynn ducked her head and moved quickly inside. Smart move, and one Ariana would be making as well. If either of them was caught on camera, it would all be over.

Behind Ariana, Brigit and Adam edged their way toward the door of their car. Ariana leaned over and stopped them.

"Wait."

"What's wrong?" Brigit asked.

"Tahira's just about to go through," Ariana said. "You want to be last, right? The big finale? Don't let her steal your spotlight. You know how much she'd enjoy it."

Brigit nodded and smiled. "You're right. Thanks, Ana."

"No problem."

Tahira got out of the car with Rob, and right away, all lenses were trained on the princess of Dubai. Tahira ate it up, waving, posing, flashing her wide grin, swiveling her hips. She made her way to the top of the red carpet so slowly, Ariana had to take baby steps just to get there when she wanted to—right in front of Tahira.

"Hello, everyone! Well yes, of course! Brigit and I are dear, *dear* friends!" Tahira shouted, answering reporters questions. Ariana felt like hurling. Or, at the very least, stepping on the girl's glittery gold train so she'd trip and fall on her overly made-up face. But instead she had to concentrate on walking slowly enough to get through the door just ahead of Tahira, and on making sure that none of the cameras could get a clear picture of her face.

"What're you doing, Covington?" Tahira hissed under her breath, keeping her smile on. "Trying to throw me into shadow with your big head?"

"Ah, Tahira. It would have to be *bigger* than yours to accomplish that," Ariana replied blithely.

Tahira's smile only faltered for a moment, and she went back to working the crowd. By the time they finally reached the door of the embassy, even Rob was checking his watch.

"Can we get on with this? I'm starving," he said under his breath.

"Do you think of nothing other than your stomach?" Tahira snapped. "This is practically my *job*, you know. I have an image to maintain."

"I know. Sorry," Rob said, chagrined. He lifted his hands in surrender as the line edged forward.

"Omigod, Rob, did I tell you? I got the *best* dirt on a donor," Tahira said out of nowhere. The hairs on the back of Ariana's neck prickled.

"Really?" Rob whispered. Clearly Tahira had broken the rules and told him all about Stone and Grave *and* her secret task. Ariana wondered if the Stone and Grave members knew about this. Or if there was some way she could let them know.

Of course, after tonight, it wouldn't matter anymore that Tahira had broken the rules.

"What is it?" Rob asked.

"I'll tell you later," Tahira said. Then she leaned toward Ariana's ear from behind. "But somebody's going daaa-own!" she sang under her breath.

It took every ounce of Ariana's willpower to keep from turning around and smacking the girl across the face.

She had to go. It was either her or Ariana. Simple as that. Ariana arrived at the front of the line.

"Please place any metal objects in the container on the belt, then move through," the guard instructed.

Ariana had nothing metal on her person, so she slipped through the gate with no problem. Up ahead, revelers were gathering in a huge anteroom, partaking in champagne and appetizers. Ariana hesitated, loitering among the few klatches of people who had stayed behind to chat in this first hall.

Tahira received the same instructions from the guard and, like Ariana, placed nothing on the belt. She moved through the gate in front of Rob, and Ariana held her breath. Instantly, the red light atop the arc of the gate started to blink and a discreet but irritating alarm pealed out. The key had done its job.

"Miss, would you mind stepping this way?" a middle-aged guard said to Tahira in a Norwegian accent.

"Me?" Tahira asked, annoyed.

"Yes, please. I'll need to check the contents of your bag."

Ariana pressed her lips together to keep from smiling. So far, so good.

Tahira groaned and tipped her head back dramatically. "Do you have any idea who I am?" she said, thrusting her clutch at him.

He blinked at her, his face a blank. "No. I'm afraid I do not."

Then he unceremoniously dumped her stuff out into a plastic bin. Ariana moved slowly in the direction of the door, loitering just behind the guard. She glanced down at the bin and saw a compact mirror, a tube of lip gloss, Tahira's ID, and her EpiPen. The key Ariana had planted to make the metal detector go off hadn't fallen out. It was probably wedged into the tight outside pocket, which the guard hadn't noticed yet. All the better for Ariana. He looked the things over and, finding nothing metal, turned to the second guard.

"We'll need the wand," he said.

"The what?!" Tahira screeched as the second guard approached with a metal-detecting wand. She backed up a few steps, nearly tripping on the long hem of her gown. "You are not using that thing on me. Rob! Get your ass over here!"

Rob, however, was being detained by a third guard on the other side of the metal detector, which the security team evidently did not want to use until the current situation was sorted out. The line of partygoers was starting to back up, and everyone was standing on their toes and straining their necks to see what the commotion was.

"Can't do it, sweetie!" he said in a bored voice.

"I have rights, you know!" Tahira shouted. "And I'm a dignitary's daughter, which means I have bodyguards! God, why did I tell them to stay home? If you give me my phone I can have them here in five minutes and they'll kick your scrawny Norwegian butt right back to Oslo."

"As appealing as that sounds, it's not necessary," the first guard said, approaching Tahira, who was trying to wrench her arm out of the second guard's grasp. "Now if you'll just stand still for a moment, miss. We're simply attempting to do our jobs."

"You people suck, you know that?" Tahira ranted, making an even bigger scene. So much for that image she was trying to maintain. "I don't know why we're allies with you old-school bastards. Norway sucks. In fact, Europe sucks!"

There was a general gasp from the waiting crowd, which was probably full of European dignitaries.

"Yeah, that's right! I said it!" Tahira said, still squirming. "I hate Europe!"

Now the crowd started to murmur and shout. Ariana laughed and, with both guards now fully occupied by a screeching brat and a potential revolt, she quickly grabbed Tahira's EpiPen and slipped it into her purse. Then she turned and joined the party.

Part two of her plan was complete.

THE TOUR

"Ana! Ana! Ana!"

Brigit half-scurried, half-wobbled across the crowded ballroom, forcing ladies in couture and men in tails to dodge out of her way as she went. A woman in a glittering tiara laughed in an indulgent way as the princess raced around like a girl half her age. Ariana smiled as she caught Brigit in her arms before she could fall forward in her high heels. It must have been nice to have an entire country looking after you, indulging you, like you were a favorite daughter.

"What? What is it?" Ariana asked with a laugh, clutching Brigit's elbows as Brigit clutched hers.

"I did it! I did my task!" Brigit whispered breathlessly, her chest heaving up and down.

"You embarrassed the crown prince of Jordan?" Ariana replied under her breath. "How?"

"I was standing with him and Prince William and a couple of the senators' sons and I said I smelled dog poo and I made them all take off their shoes to check, which of course they did because I'm the princess and when you're within these walls you pretty much have to do whatever I say," Brigit rambled, leading Ariana toward a velvet bench near the wall and dropping down. "That was pretty much all I had to do," she said, lifting her palms and laughing.

"Make him take off his shoes? How is that embarrassing?" Ariana asked, setting her empty champagne glass down on the table next to her. It was immediately whisked away by a white-gloved waiter.

"Because the crown prince of Jordan wears *lifts*," Brigit whispered conspiratorially. "When he took off his shoes he was at least three inches shorter, and now all the guys know! You should have seen the look on his face. I thought Will was going to die laughing."

"Wow. You are evil," Ariana said jokingly.

"I know, right?" Brigit said, holding her hand over her mouth. "Maybe I should have asked *him* to teach me how to walk in these heels." She tugged her skirt up slightly to show off her sparkly shoes. "Can I take them off yet?" she whimpered. "I swear I almost took down one of the tapestries back there just trying to bow to that guy from the Japanese embassy."

"No. You are not removing the shoes," Ariana said, placing a calming hand on Brigit's arm. "You're doing fine. It's only a few hours."

Brigit rolled her eyes just as Kaitlynn appeared with Lexa, Conrad, Adam, and Soomie in tow.

"Brigit, this party is amazing," Kaitlynn said, her face flushed with pleasure.

"Eh. It's okay," Brigit said with a shrug.

"And this building is beautiful," Kaitlynn added, looking around at the high ceilings. "Would you mind giving us a tour? I mean, of whatever parts we're allowed to see?" she added with an endearingly self-deprecating laugh.

"Sure," Brigit said, reaching her arms out to Kaitlynn for help. Kaitlynn hoisted Brigit up onto her heels as gracefully as possible. "You coming, Ana?"

"I'm in," Ariana replied. Even though she had assured Kaitlynn countless times that she was taking care of the Stone and Grave situation, she still didn't relish the thought of leaving Kaitlynn alone with any of her friends. "Let's do it."

Brigit took the lead with Adam and Lexa; Conrad and Kaitlynn fell in behind them. Along the way they picked up Soomie, Christian, and a few other APH students who wanted to get in on the exclusive tour. Palmer hung back and waited for Ariana to join him.

"Hey," Ariana said, her heart fluttering at his close proximity. "Having fun?"

"Yeah. I'd be having more fun if I had a date," he replied lightly.

"Palmer, I thought you understood," Ariana replied. "I need to fly under the radar for now."

"What's the big deal?" Palmer asked. "People break up and start dating other people all the time."

"Yeah, but not best friends," Ariana replied as Brigit led them across the lobby and through a pair of double doors on the other side.

"How can you guys be best friends? Until two weeks ago you hadn't even spoken in years," Palmer whispered.

Ariana's heart turned. How could Palmer question her and Lexa's connection? Did Lexa not want to be her best friend? Had she said something to Palmer about her before they broke up that implied that she didn't really like Ariana?

"Don't be mean," Ariana replied firmly.

Palmer blew out a sigh. "I'm sorry. I just . . . I want to be able to be with you, that's all." He glanced ahead at the rest of the tour group, slowing his steps to put some distance between them. "I want to be able to do this." He lifted her hand and kissed her wrist lightly, looking right into her eyes. Her entire body actually shivered, which made Palmer smile.

"You can do that all you want," she whispered. "Later."

"Promise?" Palmer asked with a sexy smile.

Ariana grinned. "Promise."

They would just have to find someplace private for him to do it.

Brigit was explaining the origin of some Renaissance-style painting as Ariana and Palmer caught up. Then she turned toward the back of the mansion and threw open another pair of doors, so tall they practically reached the ceiling.

"Whoa," Adam said, his eyes wide as they stepped into a huge room with a broad, winding staircase at the center. There were ladders and scaffolding positioned all around the room, and white paint peeled from the domed ceiling overhead.

"They usually hold the NoBash in this room, but as you can see, it's under construction," Brigit said, her heels clipping at an uneven pace as she crossed toward the staircase. "I'll show you guys my dad's office upstairs. He still has my nursery set up next door and it's just the way it was when I was a baby."

She started up the steps, holding the skirt of her gown up with one hand and clinging to the oak railing with the other. Her heel caught on the carpet about halfway up and she stopped, took a breath, and kept going.

"You sure I can't take off the shoes yet?" she asked Ariana, glancing over her shoulder.

"Not yet!" Lexa, Soomie, Kaitlynn, and Ariana all chorused, then laughed.

Brigit shook her head and pointed out a few more paintings and tapestries as they ascended the stairs. Ariana was impressed with all the knowledge she had accrued about the various artists and their styles. Brigit was a girl of many layers. Ariana liked that in a person.

"Can you believe this place?" Kaitlynn said to Ariana and Palmer, waiting for them to catch up. She eyed the paintings with a covetous glean in her eye. "It's all so beautiful."

Ariana wondered what she was really thinking. Was she planning on trying to lift one of these priceless works of art? The girl would never even get out the front door with it. But the idea got Ariana wondering . . . what exactly *was* Kaitlynn's task for Stone and Grave? Was it something that was supposed to happen tonight, specifically, like Brigit's had been?

She hoped it wasn't anything that would get Kaitlynn arrested. Because if it was, they were both going down.

"Oh, look at this one, Ana," Kaitlynn said, pausing at the top of the stairs in front of a painting of two cherubs. Ariana stopped and shot Palmer a look that told him she'd catch up with him and the rest of the group. He strolled ahead slowly, keeping himself between Ariana and Kaitlynn and the rest. Clearly, he had no interest in being with anyone else. The thought made Ariana's heart flutter.

"It's great," Ariana said to Kaitlynn through her teeth. "Can we go now?"

"I just wanted to check in with you about your plan," Kaitlynn said, looking at the painting with feigned interest. "You do realize that tonight is your deadline."

"Believe me, I know," Ariana replied. She glanced back down the stairs, thinking of the ballroom. Realizing she really should get back there and get the deed done already. "I told you not to worry. I've got it all under control."

Kaitlynn slipped a sideways glance at Ariana. "You'd better." Then she looked past Ariana at her friends, who were just starting to crowd into a room at the end of the hall. "Because if you don't, what happens next is all on you."

NECESSARY

Tahira stood at the center of the ballroom, stopping every waiter who passed by and hoarding hors d'oeuvres like they were the last morsels of food on earth. Ariana had seen the girl eat before, and knew she was a glutton. It was a key element of her plan. But watching her now made Ariana's stomach turn. The girl was so slovenly, so rude, so unworthy of her position. Ariana was about to do the world a favor, really. No one needed a girl like this flitting around the globe pretending to be a role model.

The door to the hallway opened, the door from which the waiters had been emerging all night, and Ariana spotted a handsome, college-age guy in a white tuxedo jacket and tails weaving his way toward her. Ariana had been studying the waiters' movements for the last fifteen minutes or so and understood the intricate dance of their circuit. If she was right, this one would work his way along the north wall, where she was standing, then veer toward the center of the room when he hit the bar. Veer toward Tahira, Zuri, and Rob.

It was now or never. Ariana slipped the small vial of peanut oil from her purse, stepped away from the wall, and stood in front of the waiter.

"Hi," she said with a bright smile.

He looked her up and down and smiled in return. "Good evening, miss. Would you like a canapé?"

Ariana was glad that Palmer and the rest of her friends were out on the verandah somewhere, taking in the view of the city. At least no one had to see her flirting with the help. Not to mention poisoning their classmate.

"Sure," Ariana said, plucking one from his silver tray. "But I really just came over here to tell you that your shoe is untied."

"Oh, thanks," he said, placing his tray down on the end of the bar behind her. "I guess it would be bad if I tripped and showered all the dignitaries with canapés."

"Probably," Ariana replied, her heart pounding.

As soon as the waiter crouched down, Ariana turned and dumped the peanut oil all over the canapés. By the time he had realized neither of his shoes was, in fact, untied, and stood up again, Ariana was looking in the other direction as if nothing had happened.

"Nope. I'm good," he said.

"Huh. I could have sworn I saw a shoelace trailing behind you," Ariana said, lifting a shoulder as he picked up his tray. "Maybe it was one of the other waiters."

"I'll keep an eye out," he said in a friendly way. "Enjoy the party, miss."

"Thanks. I definitely will," she replied.

Especially if you go where I'm hoping you'll go right now, she added silently.

Sure enough, the waiter hooked a left and headed toward Tahira and her friends. A few people grabbed canapés from his tray along the way, but there were plenty left when Tahira reached up to select one from the tray.

"There are no peanuts in this, right?" Ariana heard her ask, just as she'd been doing all night. "Because I am deathly allergic."

"No, miss. No peanuts," the waiter replied.

Ariana was surprised by the lump that formed in her throat as Tahira brought the hors d'oeuvre to her lips.

This has to happen, she told herself. *It's the only way. She threatened you. Threatened to expose you. And once she's gone, you, Kaitlynn, and Brigit will all sail through and into Stone and Grave. This is the only way to protect yourself and to make sure Kaitlynn gets everything she wants.*

Tahira popped the canapé into the gaping maw of her mouth and crunched down. Almost instantly, her eyes widened and her hand went to her throat.

"Tahira? What is it? Are you choking?" Zuri cried.

Tahira shook her head wildly. Her hair tumbled free from its updo as she shoved her bag at Rob. "Pen . . . EpiPen."

The people around them started to back away in fear and disgust, forming a small circle of open floor around the trio. Ariana endeavored to swallow but found that she couldn't. She could hardly watch this, but she also found that she couldn't look away.

"Oh, shit. She ate peanut," Rob said, fumbling into her bag. He pawed through it as Tahira lurched forward, bent over at the waist. "It's not here!"

Tahira's eyes bulged. Clearly, she could no longer speak. People in the crowd were murmuring, alarmed. Ariana heard someone ask for a doctor. No one moved.

"What?" Zuri cried, clinging to her friend's arm. "It has to be! She always has it!"

"You think I don't know that?" Rob dropped to his knees and dumped the purse out on the floor. "It's not here!"

Tahira's knees hit the floor and Zuri let out a strangled cry.

Ariana closed her eyes and turned her head, her throat tightening. What was wrong with her? This had to happen. Why was she being so dramatic?

"Omigod! Help!" Zuri screamed. "We need a doctor! Someone help!"

Ariana took a breath. It was always difficult to watch someone die. Even those people who deserved it. Of course she was upset. But this was necessary. They had all been necessary.

"Please! Please, help her!" Zuri cried, tears streaming down her face as Tahira choked and gasped. "Call nine-one-one!"

Finally, a few people shoved through the crowd. A wiry gentleman with white hair raced forward and grabbed Tahira's wrist, checking her pulse. Ariana held her breath. She found she didn't know what to hope for.

"An allergic reaction?" he asked.

"Do something! She can't breathe!" Zuri cried.

"She needs an EpiPen," Rob said, getting up from the floor. "Does anyone have an EpiPen?" he shouted, wheeling around. The ladies and gentlemen in the crowd looked at him like he was a lion on a rampage. "Someone here has to have one."

"Here!"

Suddenly Ariana's bag was ripped from her grasp. Kaitlynn yanked out the EpiPen and, without a second glance at Ariana, rushed toward Tahira, who was now prone on the floor, her eyes rolling back in her head. Kaitlynn handed the pen to the doctor, who quickly exposed the needle and shoved it into Tahira's arm.

Ariana watched all this as if it was happening in slow motion. Her plan was going up in smoke, with Kaitlynn lighting the fire beneath it. She couldn't breathe, couldn't move, couldn't feel a thing other than despair. The room started to blur around her, everyone moving in slow motion.

Why? Why was Kaitlynn doing this? The girl had been about to get exactly what she wanted. Ariana knew that Tahira's friendship couldn't mean that much to her. No one had ever meant that much to Kaitlynn. So what the hell was she doing?

Soon Tahira was breathing again. Rob and Zuri carefully helped her sit up. She held her throat, which was undoubtedly strained from all the choking.

"Are you okay?" Rob asked.

Tahira nodded. "What happened?" she croaked.

"This young lady here saved your life," the doctor said, gesturing up at Kaitlynn. "She found an EpiPen just in time."

With Zuri and Rob's help, Tahira struggled to her feet. Then she threw herself at Kaitlynn, clinging to her with her arms around her neck.

"Thank you. Thank you, thank you, thank you," she croaked.

Everyone in the immediate vicinity started to applaud, and soon the whole room and its hundreds of revelers were cheering and clapping for Kaitlynn's achievement.

"Get that girl a drink!" someone shouted, earning laughter from the crowd.

"It was nothing," Kaitlynn replied modestly. "I have allergies too, so I always have one on me," she said, glancing meaningfully over at Ariana. "Anyone would have done the same."

Ariana finally breathed in. Interesting. So she hadn't done it so that she could tell everyone that Ariana had stolen Tahira's EpiPen.

"Come on," Rob said, putting his arm around Tahira's waist. "I think we should get you checked out."

"He's right. I'd like to gauge your blood pressure and make sure you're all right," the doctor said. "There's an emergency kit at the front."

Tahira had one arm around Rob's shoulders and the other around the doctor's as they passed by Ariana on their way to the door. Zuri scurried after them, holding both her purse and Tahira's. And Kaitlynn, who was trailed by a smattering of applause, brought up the rear. As she walked by Ariana, she lifted Ariana's wrist and slapped something into her hand. Then she smirked, and followed her friends.

Slowly, her fingers quaking, Ariana unfolded the scrap of black paper—Kaitlynn's task. It read, in silver lettering:

BE THE HERO.

NEXT

Ariana Osgood was at a loss. Her plan had failed, foiled by the very person for whom she had created said plan in the first place. Now, all she could think about was what Kaitlynn had said at the top of the stairs during their tour of the embassy.

What happens next is on you.

What was going to happen next? As of this moment, Ariana had no idea. And that thought terrified her more than anything.

She stood near the wall of the ballroom, watching Kaitlynn as she chatted and laughed with Tahira, Zuri, and Allison, who were now solidified for life as her bestest best friends.

Be the hero, Ariana thought. What would Kaitlynn have done if Ariana hadn't tried to take out Tahira? If Ariana had tossed the EpiPen? Probably put Ariana in some kind of mortal danger and then saved her at the last minute. Or someone else. They were all just pawns in the girl's sadistic game.

Kaitlynn laughed at something Tahira said, and Ariana's eyes narrowed. The real question was, what was the girl thinking? How was she going to create a spot for herself in Stone and Grave? What sort of plan was percolating in that distorted little mind of hers?

"Hey."

Palmer's breath on her bare shoulder sent a pleasant shot of warmth down her spine, totally incongruous with the cold fear that permeated every other inch of her.

"Hey," she replied, standing up straight and trying to smile.

"Apparently I missed some serious drama," Palmer said, taking a sip of his drink, some sort of dark brown liquid. Ariana eyed it with interest. Perhaps it was time for her to get silly drunk. To just let herself go and let whatever was going to happen, happen. Her brain was starting to hurt from the strain of trying to protect everyone. Of trying to make sense of a senseless psycho.

"Yeah. Lily saved the day," Ariana said airily. "No wonder you can't seem to stop flirting with her."

Palmer looked down at his feet, chagrined. "Not by choice."

"What's that supposed to mean?" Ariana asked, tearing her gaze from Kaitlynn for just a moment.

"She's always coming up to me," he said, finishing his drink and placing the tumbler on the empty tray of a passing waiter. "And yeah, maybe I don't spend too much effort fighting her off, but there's a chance that I'm just hoping to make you jealous."

Ariana's eyebrows arched. "Really?"

"Is it working?" Palmer asked with a grin.

Ariana took in a breath, let it go, and sank against Palmer's strong chest. She was done. Exhausted. Sick of keeping up appearances on top of everything else. At the moment, for just *one* moment, she really just needed a hug. The feeling of a pair of strong, reassuring arms holding her. Letting her know that everything was going to work out in the end.

"Whoa," Palmer said, circling his arms around her. She closed her eyes and cuddled into his warmth. "What's this? What about flying under the radar?"

"Lexa's happy with Connie," Ariana replied. "I don't see why I don't get to be happy too."

"Finally got through to you, huh?" Palmer joked, brushing a stray lock of hair back from her face, tickling her cheek.

"I guess you did," she replied.

"No worries," Palmer said. "Lexa's not around anyway. I haven't seen her since before the big near-death scene, actually."

Ariana's heart careened to a screeching stop. Her eyes popped open. Lexa was missing? Missing *before* Tahira was saved by the one person who wanted to create a hole in the secret society?

"I bet she and Conrad are off hooking up in one of the upstairs rooms," Palmer whispered, moving his hands up to cup her cheeks. "In fact, maybe we could go find a room of our own."

Ariana took a step back. Her knees trembled beneath her. "Lexa's missing?"

A look of confusion crossed Palmer's face. "I didn't say missing."

"No, but . . ." Ariana brought her hand to her forehead, trying to ease her suddenly racing thoughts. "You haven't seen her. Has anyone seen her? Where's Conrad?"

"I don't know," Palmer said, reaching for her hand. "I'm sure they're around here somewhere. Now why don't we—"

"No." Ariana wrenched her arm free. "I have to go."

"Now?" Palmer was no longer confused. He was pissed. But Ariana couldn't deal with that now. Kaitlynn had done something to Lexa. She could feel it in her bones.

"Yes, now. I have to find Lexa," Ariana told him.

"What is it with you and her?" Palmer blurted, backing up a step. "It's like you're in love with *her.*"

"Palmer! I don't have time to stroke your ego right now," Ariana said. "I have to go."

She turned and raced out of the ballroom, heading back for the lobby so she could talk to the guards. Maybe Lexa and Conrad had simply bailed. Perhaps one of the guards would remember them leaving.

Please don't let her be hurt, Ariana thought as she raced along in her heels, holding up her skirt at both sides. *If she is, it's all my fault. I was supposed to protect my friends.*

It was a lesson she had learned back at Billings. A lesson that had been drilled into her time and again. And here at APH, it was even more vital than ever. Because Ariana was the one who had brought Kaitlynn here. Ariana should have been more diligent. She should have figured out a better way to shield them from Kaitlynn's twisted nature. If Lexa was dead, Ariana was to blame.

"Excuse me!" Ariana shouted, racing up to the first guard she saw. "Have you seen a girl . . . a bit taller than me . . . dark hair in a green dress? She was with an African-American guy. . . ."

"Omigod! Ana!"

Ariana whirled around at the sound of Lexa's voice. Her lungs filled with relief. She was there. Right there. Running toward Ariana at full tilt with tears streaming down her face.

Tears.

Just like that, the relief was gone.

"Lexa! What is it!?" Ariana said turning as her friend barreled into her. Conrad brought up the rear, his face slack, his eyes wide with fright.

"I . . . I . . . I can't . . . !" Lexa choked, barely able to breathe.

"What!?"

Lexa collapsed forward and Ariana was unable to hold her full weight. She sank to the floor on her knees, the skirt of her dress ballooning around her. Ariana stepped around her and numbly staggered toward the doors through which Lexa and Conrad had come.

What did Kaitlynn do? What's happening? Ariana thought as she stepped through the doors to the tapestry room. Her gaze instantly focused on the heap of purple lying at the foot of the grand staircase. On the silver high-heeled shoe lying several feet away. On the tangle of blond hair.

"Oh my God," Ariana gasped, bending over at the waist. Suddenly there was no air, like the tapestries were suffocating the room and Ariana along with it. "Brigit."

The princess's eyes were closed, like she was sleeping peacefully. She could have been. If not for the odd, unnatural angle of her neck.

A single tear spilled down Ariana cheek. "Brigit, I'm so . . . so sorry."

Just then, the guards rushed through on either side of Ariana, whipping guns from holsters and holding walkie-talkies to their mouths. As a few of them crouched to the floor around Brigit's lifeless form, Ariana was quickly ushered out by a pair of firm hands—ushered back to the lobby where Lexa and Conrad now sat on a pair of chairs, being grilled by still more guards.

"At the bottom of the stairs," Lexa was saying as Ariana slowly approached. "I think she fell. . . . She must've tripped or . . ." Her eyes suddenly widened and she looked up at Ariana, past the square shoulder of one of the guards. "Why did we make her wear those stupid heels?"

Ariana swallowed against her dry throat, her heart breaking. *It's not your fault, Lexa. It's not your fault.*

Soon, a crowd started to form in the lobby. The news traveled quickly and the Norwegian ambassador was brought forth. She was ushered through the double doors and disappeared. Her shriek of despair was soon heard throughout the embassy.

"You found the princess?" a tall man in a suit asked Lexa, stepping next to the guards.

Conrad stood up. "We both did."

"You'll have to come with me," the man said.

Lexa stood up shakily. Ariana gave her a quick hug as she and

Conrad trailed after the man. Then Ariana was left standing there, alone and cold, wishing she could turn back time. Wishing she had spent every moment of the evening with Brigit. Wishing she could, at the very least, apologize. Say good-bye.

Why did it have to be her? The sweetest of the sweet? The most innocent of them all? She had been the most thoughtful, the most loyal among them.

Ariana felt a cold hand on her shoulder. She turned around and stared into Kaitlynn's dancing green eyes. If the girl could have comprehended the ferocity of the rage bubbling just beneath the thin veneer of Ariana's skin, she never could have smiled at her the way she was smiling now.

"What did you do?" Ariana said through her teeth.

"Told you, Ana," Kaitlynn whispered merrily. "This one's on you."